WENDY KREMER

KISS ME, KATE

Complete and Unabridged

LINFORD
Leicester

First published in Great Britain in 2018

First Linford Edition
published 2020

A catalogue record for this book is available
from the British Library.

ISBN 978–1–4448–4580–8

Published by
Ulverscroft Limited
Anstey, Leicestershire

Set by Words & Graphics Ltd.
Anstey, Leicestershire
Printed and bound in Great Britain by
TJ Books Limited, Padstow, Cornwall

This book is printed on acid-free paper

KISS ME, KATE

When Kate Parker begins work as the new secretary at a domestic head hunting company, the last thing she expects is to fall for her boss! Ryan Hayes, who runs the firm with his uncle, is deliciously appealing. But beautiful and elegant Louise seems to have a prior claim to him, and what man could resist her charms? Plus an old flame makes an appearance in Kate's life. Could she and Ryan have a future together — especially after Louise comes out with a shock announcement?

Chalk and Cheese

When he opened the door and saw an unknown woman seated behind the desk in their outer office, he blinked for a fraction of a second before he walked purposely towards her.

'Good morning.'

She glanced at him briefly.

'Good morning,' she replied. 'Can I help you?' She then focused on a dog-eared notebook, and riffled through the pages. 'Do you have an appointment?' Running her finger down the grubby page for the day, she frowned.

'Mr Jackson hasn't arrived yet and I don't think he'll have time to see you, when he does.' Kate already knew, after just a few days, that Hugh wouldn't let an unannounced client corner him for attention.

She looked up, and examined the

stranger more closely. He was very tall and good-looking. His top-quality business suit fitted his slim figure to perfection and his firm features and the set of his shoulders declared he was someone who had plenty of self-confidence.

He was the kind of man that her best friend Christine would describe as deliciously appealing. She mused that she liked men who knew what they wanted from life, too, but that didn't make them easy companions.

Her last boyfriend had been easy-going, but she found out that he lacked character. He quit their relationship as soon as he felt threatened by Kate's unexpected responsibilities.

Suddenly, she realised the man was talking to her and she quickly shelved her wandering thoughts and concentrated on the conversation.

'I presume you're the new secretary?' The corner of his mouth twitched fleetingly, and although Kate couldn't imagine why, she was glad, because it softened his features.

'I expect you've discovered that Hugh is chaotic and disorganised,' he continued. 'He also avoids office appointments like the plague. He prefers the setting of a good restaurant, or the bar of a renowned hotel.'

Ryan eyed the shining hair and jade coloured eyes, and mused that Hugh had engaged a looker this time. What he could see of her, told him she had a slim figure with curves in the right places.

The previous secretary had reminded him of his strict French teacher at grammar school. He'd guessed when he saw that woman at the time that she wouldn't last long.

She had a clockwork brain, and methodical methods. She had tried to reform Hugh's ways of working and openly disapproved of his easy-going attitude. It was a complete mystery why Hugh couldn't find a secretary who lasted longer than a few weeks.

They were one of the best recruiting

3

agencies in the UK and Hugh was extremely good at finding office staff for other people.

Ryan viewed this young woman more carefully and noted her gentle, accommodating expression. Hugh might be luckier this time.

For a brief moment, Kate felt annoyed because he seemed to know Hugh well. She didn't know who this man was. But an efficient secretary wouldn't be lost for words.

'As a matter of fact, yes, I am the new secretary. May I ask who you are?'

He moved towards one of the inner doors.

'I'm Hayes, Ryan Hayes. I'm the other half of Jackson and Hayes. What's your name?'

'Kate . . . Kate Parker.' She coloured as she replied. Hugh had told her there was another partner but nothing more than that, and she'd seen no photos.

'As this is the first time we've met,' she added, flustered, 'I hope you'll understand why I didn't recognise you.

I only started here two days ago.'

She hadn't seen much of Hugh, because he was out most of the time. She was getting used to his hurried comings and goings. When she started, he'd gestured to the various bundles of papers and folders piled on her desk, and the general disorder everywhere, and told her to 'sort it out'.

Apart from noting telephone messages, and the name of anyone who wanted to speak to him urgently, he'd left her to her own devices. He did give her his telephone number but only for urgent matters. To strangers he seemed vague and disorganised, but she could tell he was on top of his job.

He knew everyone in the field of domestic head hunting, and had fantastic connections in all the right places. When he interviewed people, his friendly, jovial character soon put them at ease and later his opinion about their ability was always spot-on.

She'd seen letters thanking him for sending them a very suitable employee.

Until now, she'd presumed that the second name on the door might even be fictitious.

Ryan Hayes turned and glanced at the coffee machine. His eyebrows lifted.

'Is there a chance of coffee?'

She nodded.

'I was just going to make it.'

Without further comment, he disappeared into his office.

The coffee tray had a chipped sugar bowl filled with dubious-looking sugar, a container with powdered milk, and a couple of unattractive mugs. At least the coffee was good. It came from a machine.

She decided the coffee situation was one thing more that needed to be upgraded. She'd bring some unwanted mugs from home tomorrow.

She knocked on his door. He looked at her briefly and his eyes skimmed the tray.

'Just a mug of black coffee, no milk, no sugar — and I don't expect you to wait on me from now on. I'll fetch my own whenever I feel like it.'

She put the mug on the side of the desk. Kate had clipped her hair back behind her ears that morning. Wisps had escaped and caressed her cream cheeks.

The movement of his hand as he reached out for the mug drew her attention to his long fingers with their neat nails. He'd loosened his tie and rolled up his shirtsleeves.

She turned away and wished she'd chosen something smarter to wear than her high-street-bought black slacks and simple white blouse.

'You haven't messed about with the printer's settings, I hope? I want to print some letters.'

'No, I haven't even switched it on yet. I haven't needed to, ever since I arrived. I don't know if Hugh is using pigeon post, but he definitely doesn't write many letters.'

Ryan swallowed his laughter.

'Putting pen to paper has never been Hugh's strong point. You'll have to prod him if you think a return letter is indispensable. I do write letters, and I need to print them out.

'Oh, by the way, don't ever change any print setting on your computer. We are all in the same network, and the printer settings should be the same for everyone.

'The last woman Hugh employed thought she would improve things. She messed up the system and it took me ages to sort it out again. Hugh's afraid of computers — that's another reason why he doesn't write many letters. He prefers to phone.'

Kate nodded and glanced at him briefly again before she left. He was already busy with the work spread out on his desk. She went out and realised the second partner was a completely different kettle of fish. He was young, quite attractive, and had a distinct air of authority.

Back at her desk, she switched on the computer and printer. She ransacked the muddle in the so-called stationery cupboard to find a new and clean folder for his letters.

The printer threw out various crisp, neatly typed pages. She patted them into order and put them in the folder. She was about to take them in to Ryan Hayes when the office door opened and Hugh came in.

Hugh was mid-fifties, with a ruddy complexion, twinkling blue eyes and bushy eyebrows. His nose was short and straight and his mouth turned up at the corners. It meant that his features had a permanently friendly appearance.

His salt and pepper hair needed trimming. He was wearing a moss-coloured tweed jacket with leather elbow patches, corduroy trousers, a checked shirt, and a tie that boasted that he was a member of a well-known golf club.

He sauntered across, smiled and put down a paper bag with a bakery emblem. He glanced at the piles of paper on her desk, removed a folded newspaper from under his arm and tapped it against his legs.

'Morning, my dear! That looks daunting,' he commented. 'I hope I don't have to check it all?'

'No, unless I can't match them.' She indicated the nearest-pile. 'That one is contracts you've signed and the other is the bank accounts for commission payments for the signed contracts. At the moment they don't all correspond with each other, so their counterparts are probably among things I haven't yet checked.'

She gestured to the third pile.

'That one is enquiries from applicants asking you to represent them. I don't know if you have followed them up or not, so I kept them. There are also some completed forms from prospective clients. Most of them are completely out of date.'

His eyebrows lifted, and he nodded.

'Good! Good! It all sounds pretty awful to me.' His brows furrowed as he eyed another large pile on the floor next to the desk. 'I hope that's rubbish?'

'Yes. Junk mail you've received through the post. I didn't know if you wanted to check it.'

'Heaven forbid! Throw it away. I'm not interested. I'll leave it up to you . . . ' He looked at his watch. 'Any messages?' Kate handed him a list. His eyes explored the contents.

'Umm . . . I'll sort these out this afternoon. I'm due for lunch with an old client in an hour's time, and I'm looking forward to it. He's chosen a delightful restaurant — expensive, but wonderful food. Anything else happened I should know about?'

'Mr Hayes arrived a short time ago.'

He looked slightly bewildered.

'Ryan? I wasn't expecting him this week. Is he in his office?'

'Yes. I was just about to give him this folder with his letters.'

Hugh held out his hand.

'I'll take it. Did you introduce yourself?'

Kate looked at him steadily and nodded.

11

'He seemed very surprised to find me here.'

'Hmm. I expect he was. I haven't spoken to him for a couple of days, and he wouldn't know that you've joined us. I forgot to mention it. Not that it will surprise him very much.

'We've had a few secretaries over the last couple of months,' he admitted, 'and he gave up trying to remember their names and faces. In fact, he started complaining about it. I don't know why it bothers him, considering he's hardly ever in the office himself.'

'Perhaps he expects efficient help when he is here. If you've had difficulty finding the right person so far, he could think I'm unsuitable too,' Kate pointed out.

'Nonsense! In fact, to be honest, you are over-qualified for the job. We've never had an accountant doing our office work before. You're not thinking of leaving us already, are you? You've only been here a couple of days. I say . . . I haven't done, or said, something

12

wrong, have I, Kate?'

'No, of course not! It is just that your partner is completely different.'

He gestured elaborately with his hand.

'Ryan is efficiency personified, but he never argues about how I organise the office. He handles all his own work and sometimes I think he only sees this place as a convenient and suitable address for his business card.'

Kate swallowed and glanced briefly at the untidy piles of papers, folders, and general disorderly clutter spread throughout the room. Hugh's room was even worse — if that was possible.

She was silent for a moment.

'I think it's because Mr Hayes has a completely different business approach than you do,' she said tactfully.

Hugh laughed gruffly.

'You can say that again. I must give him his due, though. He gets things done. He's my nephew. Did you know that? We're as different as chalk and cheese.

'My sister Sally is like Ryan. Never anything out of place, never a dirty dish in the sink, everything recorded, listed, and organised. My flat is like a chaotic charity shop most of the time, even though I have a jewel of a cleaning lady.'

Kate could imagine what his flat was like. His cleaner must be very adaptable and accommodating. It didn't matter. Kate liked Hugh. She admired the way he drifted through life. He seemed to have numerous close friends, knew more people than anyone else she'd ever met, and he was always cheerful.

'Don't worry about Ryan,' he continued. 'I have the feeling we'll all get on fine. If you can tidy up this place, you'll save me no end of work, impress Ryan, and be worth your weight in gold.'

Kate smiled at him.

'I'll do my best.' She handed him the folder.

He nodded towards the paper bag.

'For you and me. I didn't expect Ryan, so hide those or he'll scoff the lot in the wink of an eye. I'll just say hello, and then we'll share the doughnuts.'

His eyes twinkled and Kate found it intriguing that the two men had such completely different attitudes. It functioned, though, otherwise it would not be such a successful and profitable agency.

The agency's domestic and international reputation was impeccable. There was definitely more to this partnership than met the eye and she wanted to stay here.

Apart from needing the money badly, the office was close to an underground station and getting to and from her job was straightforward, with just one change.

Kate heard him chatting as he went into Ryan's office.

'Ryan, what a surprise! I thought you were still in Paris trying to persuade that stage director that Covent Garden would fade into disrepute unless he agreed to take over.'

The sound of murmuring and

occasional burst of laughter continued behind the closed door.

Kate concentrated on sorting papers again. It looked like it would be difficult to get Hugh to inspect anything. Hoping that he'd be interested in anything other than urgent or projected business deals was an illusion.

Ryan Hayes must be handling all his paperwork himself. She hadn't come across anything of importance addressed to him so far, just items of junk mail.

Her thoughts darkened when she thought about the untouched backlog of bookkeeping, and wondered if anyone had kept track of anything at all. Even if there were some bank statements, so far she'd found few items on overheads, expenses, payments, or office stationery.

She vowed that somehow she'd get things back into shape. It would take time, but she'd never shirked a challenge yet, and this office was certainly a challenge.

16

She would need to be diplomatic, because Hugh didn't want to be bothered, or face any kind of questioning, but perhaps she could persuade him to help now and then. It was none of her business how chaotic his methods were.

At least Ryan Hayes seemed to have his side of the business under control.

When Hugh emerged with Ryan half-an-hour later, he'd already forgotten about their coffee break.

'We're off to that lunch date I told you about, Kate. Ryan knows him, too, and two people are more persuasive than one.' Hugh turned to his nephew. 'Ryan, you've met Kate, haven't you?'

Ryan eyed her.

'Yes, we've met.'

'Good, good! No more Mr Hayes, this is Ryan. Mr is only for outsiders.'

Kate nodded. She watched them as they went towards the door. Hugh lifted his hand in farewell. Ryan Hayes had preceded him out and already disappeared.

Kate made herself a cup of coffee and munched her way through one of the doughnuts. Brushing sugar away from the corner of her mouth, she thought how the arrival of Ryan Hayes had changed the office atmosphere completely. She wasn't sure if she liked that or not.

Glamorous Stranger

Kate got used to Ryan's lanky figure appearing and disappearing. They usually passed the time of day, but not much more. He was polite and had accepted that she was the new secretary but he never asked what she was doing, or expected her to work for him.

She transferred any telephone calls when someone asked for him, gave him the post addressed to him, and very occasionally did copying jobs but, in general, he managed all his own work.

She presumed it was because he'd got used to the unpredictability of a secretary being available in the office.

One morning he stood looking at some green plants on top of the filing cabinets and scrutinised the rest of the room.

'This place is beginning to look a lot tidier than it has for years, and I like the fact that you've added some greenery. Makes all the difference to visitors. I hope you didn't pay for those plants out of your own pocket?'

She was surprised that he'd noticed.

'No, we had too many bunched together on the window-sill at home. They have a lot more room here.'

He nodded.

'Is there any chance of coffee?' he asked before he turned towards his office.

'It's in the making. Oh, by the way, has Hugh told you that he wants to talk to you about that chef he met yesterday? I think he's querying the man's qualifications. He'd like you to look at his papers. Some of it is in French, there's a little Spanish, and there's some Danish or Swedish. He thinks some of it might be false.'

Ryan laughed, and displayed even white teeth. Kate mused on the difference his smile made to his whole features. Then, he was even more attractive.

'Well, I can manage the French part, and I might figure out some of the Spanish, but the Danish/Swedish is no-go.'

She smiled back at him, and her green eyes twinkled.

'He's not just suspicious about the references. This man is still under thirty and the recommendations seem applicable to someone much older.'

He tilted his head to the side and there was laughter in his eyes.

'It's a wonder that Hugh even noticed it.' He shrugged. 'I know a couple of people who work in top catering. I'll check the man's CV and find out. Tell Hugh to give me the details as soon as he comes in. I'm off to Munich this afternoon and I need plenty of time to get through safety controls at the airport.'

She nodded.

'Will do! He told me yesterday that he'll be in about ten.'

'Right.' He paused. 'Did you know that only two per cent of the world's population have green eyes? You are therefore almost unique.'

'Yes, I've heard that before,' she said, surprised and a bit disconcerted that he'd noticed her eyes. 'My father used to say it was because we come from Irish roots, but I discovered that it isn't necessarily true. It all comes down to genes.'

'Well, considering your eye colour and your hair, there is a very good chance that he was right.' He gave her another hesitant smile. 'I think you're going to fit in to this mad house very well.

'Welcome, Kate! I should have said that when you first arrived but I didn't know if you'd stay or not. I hope it's not too late?'

She coloured slightly, and felt quite buoyant.

'No, it's never too late. I like it here and I'm trying to catch up with neglected work while keeping an eye on present happenings.'

He looked satisfied.

'You'll have your work cut out to keep up with Hugh sometimes, but somehow I think you'll manage.' He turned away.

He was halfway across the room when Kate spoke.

'If I can do anything to ease your workload, just say so. Lots of things can be done via the internet, and then you might not have so much to do when you return.'

He looked back.

'That's an excellent idea. I could send you letters, enquiries et cetera and you could print them, and post them straight away, couldn't you?'

She smiled.

'Perhaps you can sign some blank pages? A personal signature looks much better than one from a print out. I can then fit the text to the signature.'

He looked pleased.

'That's a good idea. I'll do that before I leave.' Nodding, he continued on his way.

The atmosphere improved noticeably

as she gradually cleared the backlog of work and kept day-to-day business running smoothly.

After badgering Hugh to fish out his expenses and any other bills from amongst the chaos in his room, she caught up with a lot of the bookkeeping.

'Our tax advisor will be delighted,' Hugh commented when she told him their accounts were up-to-date. 'He played hell last time he had to do our tax returns.'

Hugh returned from a meeting that afternoon, and handed her an opulent bunch of spring flowers.

'Not only are you the longest-lasting assistant we've had for ages, you are also the best-humoured one. I am absolutely amazed that you've already sorted out so much of the mess that was here when you arrived.'

Heartened, she buried her nose in the flowers.

'Thank you, Hugh, they're lovely. They'll brighten the place up no end. I haven't sorted everything out yet. The filing cabinets are in a deplorable state, but I can see a light at the end of the tunnel.'

'And promise you won't leave us once that's finished?' he said.

She smiled.

'No. I don't see why someone else should benefit from my work.'

He nodded, and visibly relaxed.

'Quite right. You are a good girl.'

'The only danger is that I'll get bored if there isn't enough work to keep me busy.'

He stroked his chin.

'Yes, I notice you keep asking me if I have anything extra for you to do. I know that Ryan spends a lot of his time researching through various professions he's interested in, or involved in at present. I think he uses the internet to find possible candidates. He might be glad to give you that, for instance.

'I'll mention it to him next time he comes in. I can give you more of my

25

preliminary contract work too, if you like.'

Kate seldom saw Ryan. He was always busy and a lot of his work was concerned with candidates in France or on the Continent for top jobs in catering, hotels, and management.

He e-mailed her letters to print out. She usually posted them a few hours later on her way home and wondered if he minded about being abroad so much.

★ ★ ★

A few days later, she turned and automatically straightened her navy pencil skirt and sky blue silk shirt blouse when he appeared. She was very pleased to see him.

'Hi, Kate? How are things?'

'Fine. And you?'

'Me too.' He took a quick look around and commented. 'The piles of rubbish have almost disappeared. You have been busy!'

She laughed.

'It wasn't all rubbish. Some of it was important, and needed filing properly. Sorting it out was part of my job.'

'You could have dragged your feet and taken months. Hugh wouldn't have noticed.'

Ryan had noticed the changed appearance straight away, and that was the difference between the two men. They worked in different ways and had different priorities. She moved confidently to the desk and handed him a bundle of letters.

'Your recent mail. I haven't opened it but I think most of it is junk.'

He reached out. His fingers were cool and smooth when they touched hers. She opened her mouth and shut it again, annoyed by a feeling of embarrassment as her pulse quickened. How ridiculous!

He flipped through the envelopes and nodded.

'I agree — nearly all of this is junk. He kept two letters and threw the rest in the wastepaper bin. 'In future, if you have time, sort them out for me. It isn't likely that any personal correspondence will come here.

'Sometimes clients send urgent requests but if you check my post, and think that something needs prompt attention, you could scan it and e-mail it to me. That would save me a lot of hassle.'

'Yes, of course.'

He reached into his inside pocket and put his card on the desk.

'Mobile number, and private number, plus the business addresses — just in case.'

She relished the feeling that he was beginning to trust her.

He glanced at the flowers on top of the filing cabinet, but didn't comment before he disappeared into his office, the folds of his soft coat swinging in rhythm to his long, regular strides.

When Hugh arrived and heard Ryan was in his office, he went in search of him. A few minutes later, they came out together and stopped in front of her desk.

'Get your coat, Kate,' Hugh urged. 'We are taking you out.'

Surprised, she looked up at them.

'Why?' she asked.

'You've been with us a month now. You haven't given in your notice, and you're jolly good at your job.'

She laughed.

'I'm paid for doing my work.'

His eyes twinkled and then Ryan joined in with him.

'Just think of it as a kind of bonus for coping with a mess and a disarray that was none of your making. We are ordering you to join us, and we are your bosses.'

She eyed them both, smiled and shrugged.

'In that case . . .'

They strolled to a local Italian restaurant. It only had a handful of tables. Checked red-and-white table-cloths with a red candle in the centre gave the room just the right kind of ambience. The waiter handed her a menu.

Ryan smiled and gestured towards it. 'Choose whatever you like.'

Kate forgot about price and smiled at them both.

'What a treat!' she exclaimed.

Ryan leaned forward and amusement flickered in his eyes for a moment. She was glad to know that she had won his approval. His manner told her so.

They agreed to share a plate of hors d'oeuvres. The two men took the lion's share of the olives, smoked sausage, feta cheese and marinated paprika.

The talk was general, about the day's news and a highly publicised TV programme. Ryan chose salmon with fresh vegetables and Hugh chose his favourite, ravioli.

Conversation flowed easily. Hugh brought Ryan up to date with the latest gossip about their mutual family. Kate listened with interest.

'What about you, Kate?' Hugh asked. 'What's your family like?'

She chuckled.

'Not as large or colourful as yours. I don't have any siblings. My father was an only child and my mother only has one sister, so there aren't many cousins either. The two I have are OK but I don't see them often.'

Ryan crumpled his serviette and put it on the side.

'Would you like a dessert?'

Kate shook her head.

'No, thanks.'

'What do your parents do?' Hugh asked.

'My father worked for the local council as a surveyor. He died suddenly nine months ago. My mother used to be an assistant research librarian, but my father persuaded her to give up working soon after they married. I think she regrets that now, and wishes she could go back to work again. Apart from helping financially, it would do her good mentally. She's lost confidence and I'm trying to encourage her to try.'

'I'm sorry — about your father,' Hugh said understandingly.

She nodded.

'I miss him very much. He was a lovely person and a family man. I still expect him to be there when I get home from work. It must be harder still for my mum.'

'You still live at home?' Ryan asked.

'I do at present. I used to have a two-room flat not very far from here. I loved it. I moved back in with my mother after Dad died. She was worried about whether she could afford to keep the house, so I decided to give her my rent money instead.

'She doesn't use it — it's her emergency fund. As soon as she feels secure, she wants to give it back to me. If she does find some work, I'll be able to find a place of my own again sooner.' She smiled. 'I don't mind. We get on well and I know it helps her to have me home with her at present.'

Ryan considered her carefully.

'Isn't it a bit inhibiting? You're still

young. What about friends, or boy-friends?'

'Oh, Mum's very careful not to interfere. I have a small sitting-room of my own next to my bedroom. My friends come just like before. In fact I think they come more often now, because Mum often gives us something to eat!'

She looked down and fiddled with a silver spoon.

'My ex-boyfriend couldn't cope with the situation. I think he was scared about being obliged to help with house repairs or that sort of thing, and the fact that Mum was always around.'

Hugh muttered.

'Stupid chap. Were you together long?'

'No, only a couple of months. In fact, now I'm glad we've split up. It showed me what he was really like.'

Hugh nodded.

A woman interrupted them when she stopped abruptly at their table.

'Ryan. What a nice surprise! I didn't

expect to see you in London.'

She was beautiful, tall with shoulder-length blonde hair, designer clothes, and a model figure.

Ryan stood up.

'Hello, Louise. I had to come back on business. I thought you were going to join your parents in Antibes?'

She waved perfectly manicured red-tipped fingers in a vague circle.

'Oh, you know how Daddy suddenly drops everything when he thinks business deals are more important. Mummy and I are going anyway. We went on a shopping spree this morning.

'Daddy is joining us at the end of the week. It makes no difference if we come or stay, because as you know, the house is always ready and waiting.' She fluttered her long dark lashes. 'You're welcome to join us if you have time. I've invited some other friends.' She looked at him suggestively.

Ryan stuck his hand in his pocket.

'Thanks, but at the moment I have too much to do.'

She looked at the others and Ryan remembered his manners.

'You know Hugh?' She nodded. Ryan gestured briefly in Kate's direction. 'And this is Kate. She is organising our lives back at the office. Kate . . . this is an old friend of mine, Louise Thalmy.'

'Hello!' Kate nodded.

Louise responded with a weak smile. It didn't reach her eyes.

'I bet taking care of these two is a lot of fun.'

Kate didn't know if she meant it in a sarcastic way.

'I'm coping, and in fact they are fun.' She was glad she didn't need to go into details. Hugh was always fun, Ryan was, too, when he let his guard down.

A brief awkwardness hung in the air and Louise remained standing, staring at Ryan. He finally broke the silence.

'I gather you're going somewhere?'

'Henriette is getting married next week and she's having a hen-party. I'm going there now.' He nodded. If she was waiting for a comment, she was disappointed.

'Well, I hope to see you soon, Ryan,' she finally said.

He shrugged.

'Perhaps. I've an appointment with your father soon.'

She nodded and smiled.

'Have you? What about?'

'A new manager for the branch in Dieppe.'

'Yes, he mentioned that the last one manipulated the books. The silly man hoped he'd get a rise in salary if the figures showed more profit. My father knows too much about finance to miss falsifications like that.' She looked at the tiny diamond-studded watch on her delicate wrist. 'Well, I suppose I must be off. Bye!'

She directed her farewell and last glance towards Ryan. It was clear to the others they were unimportant.

Hugh waited until she was out of hearing.

'She's after you, lad!' He grinned.

Ryan didn't comment.

'Her parents are loaded,' Hugh explained. 'They're in banking and transport, aren't they, Ryan?'

'Yes, amongst other things. I have to go, too. I have an interview in twenty minutes. I presume you are not returning to the office yet?'

Hugh leaned back comfortably.

'On target! I need a cup of coffee, and Kate to keep me company.'

Kate looked across at Hugh and smiled.

'What about phone calls in the office?'

Hugh gestured to a waiter, ordered a coffee for himself, a cappuccino for Kate.

'They'll ring back if it's important.'

Ryan laughed softly and shook his head.

'What a way to run a business! See you later, partner.'

Hugh nodded.

'Good luck! Hope you'll find the right chap for the job. You've dealt with them before, haven't you?'

'They handle a lot of European and world advertising campaigns. They can't afford to have the wrong chap in charge of security. Their ideas and campaigns, in digital or written form, are worth a fortune.

'They're willing to pay us a generous commission for the right person.' He tilted his head and directed his attention to Kate. 'Do you think you can get him back to work today, Kate?'

She shrugged and smiled.

'He's my boss. I don't intend to try!'

Hugh grinned.

'Good girl!' He eyed Ryan. 'We've found the perfect secretary,' he stated.

Ryan sighed and sauntered to the door.

Ryan to the Rescue

By the time she and Hugh finally got back to the office, it was almost time to go home. Luckily, there had been no urgent phone calls.

When she arrived next morning, Hugh was already in his office. He told her that Ryan was on his way to Dundee, to close a deal with a publishing company.

Kate noticed some research work he'd left on her desk and was pleased. Having work from him as well as Hugh made her job more interesting. Nowadays, she helped both of them by researching people and jobs, and she even picked out suitable candidates for Hugh now and then.

The following Monday morning, Ryan was back in the office. Kate had had a depressing weekend thinking about how to solve her mother's present dilemma.

She'd concluded that the only solution was to cash in some of her savings, or that her mother would have to get a loan from the bank. That might not be easy, as they'd worry about lending to someone who had no regular earnings, just a small pension.

Noticing that she gave no answering smile when he handed her some work, Ryan checked her expression again. His eyebrows rose a fraction. He turned to the coffee machine and casually filled his mug, cradling it between his hands.

He reasoned that it wasn't out of line to show interest in an employee.

'Something wrong? You look down in the dumps. Thanks for the list, by the way. It saves me a lot of work.'

Kate brushed his thanks aside. She leaned back and said.

'That's OK.'

He waited.

'Come on, what's wrong? I don't know you very well, but I can tell that something's amiss. I can't believe it has something to do with Hugh.'

She gave a shaky laugh and looked up into his face.

'No, of course not. Hugh is sweet.'

His brows lifted.

'I would never describe Hugh as sweet, but . . .'

Kate already knew he wouldn't give up, so she gave in and explained.

'My mother has a financial problem, not of her own making, and I'm worried.'

'What's it about?'

'My father borrowed some money when he modernised our house a couple of years ago. It was a private loan from someone he knew. Dad promised to repay this man in three separate payments over the course of two years, at two-and-a-half percent. Now he wants the final payment immediately.

'Mum already has most of the money put aside, but needs to top it up. She thought she had more time, and he's

41

suddenly asking for ten percent interest. It's not fair, he won't listen, and I've been trying to think of a way out.'

'Does she have a contract of some kind?'

She shook her head.

'Dad played golf with him now and then. He probably told him he was short of cash and Dad jumped at the chance when this man offered him the loan.

'Obviously, he didn't expect to have a heart attack and leave Mum with the problem of repaying the last instalment plus four times the agreed interest. It was a handshake agreement.'

Ryan nodded.

'Pity that there's nothing on paper.'

'I phoned him and told him he'd get his money. I just asked him to give my mother a month or two longer. He said I was just trying to avoid paying and he wants his money now. He even threatened with police charges. It would be his word against Dad's, and Dad isn't around any more.'

Annoyance tinged Ryan's voice.

'Let me talk to this man. Give me his name and number.'

Her eyes widened.

'It's kind of you, but it's our problem, not yours. We'll find the money somehow. Mum doesn't want to touch Dad's insurance money because she's earmarked that to pay off the mortgage.'

'Kate, give me the details,' Ryan said, looking slightly exasperated.

There was no point in arguing. He was wearing his determined expression. She ruffled through her handbag, and handed him a slip of paper.

'Mum gave me this paper, where Dad jotted down the details of what they'd agreed, with the man's name, address, and telephone number.'

He put down his mug and glanced at the paper.

'It's not far from here.' Returning to his office, he came back with his overcoat. 'If anyone calls, just tell them I'll phone back later.'

Kate was too startled to offer any real objection.

'Where are you going?'

'It sounds like he sees a chance of milking you. I know a couple of people working in that area of London who might know him. I'll phone them on the way. I can always threaten him with going public. I bet Hugh knows someone on the committee of his golf club and he'd hate anyone there knowing what he was doing.'

She heard him out in silence and then gave him a shaky smile.

'Thanks, but it won't impoverish us for ever if she has to pay ten percent instead of two-and-a-half. We'll find a way.'

He shook his head.

'His behaviour is appalling. He must know that your father died recently, and your mother is still finding her feet. He's trying to take advantage of someone weaker and shouldn't get away with it.' Without further comment, he took his mobile out of his pocket and started punching in numbers as he exited.

Kate leaned back. She mused that even if he didn't get anywhere, it was very kind of him to bother. She recognised his various expressions these days. At present, he looked extremely annoyed.

* * *

When Ryan returned, he was smiling.

'After I gently explained and then threatened him, he didn't need much more persuading. He is now satisfied if your mother pays him in three months' time, and she can forget all about any kind of percentage.'

'What?'

'Close your mouth, Kate. You look like a fish out of water.'

'You've persuaded him to forget interest charges? He's perfectly entitled to them! What did you do, break his arm?'

He smiled.

'No, nothing physical. I just mentioned the names of a few people I know, and that Hugh knows people in his golf club. He gave in without a protest.

'You can arrange to meet him with the money when you're ready, or phone him and get details of his bank account. I'd do that if I were you, then you have proof that it's paid.'

'I don't think he would have given in if you hadn't blackmailed him,' she commented.

'Tut, tut! I would define it as gentle persuasion, not blackmail!' A wide smile split his face.

Kate mused that even if he was a clever, ruthless, business person, he was also a generous-hearted man. Spontaneously she reached up and kissed his cheek.

'Thank you!'

He considered her for a moment.

'A pleasure.' He took off his coat. 'I'd better get some work done. If Hugh finds out I've just arrived and I haven't even picked up the phone yet, I'll never hear the end of it — and don't you dare tell him!'

She tilted her head and her eyes sparkled.

'That means I'm in a position to blackmail you.'

'You wouldn't have enough guts to blackmail your boss,' he muttered on his way to his office. 'You like your job too much.'

He was right. She did.

* * *

Ryan came in when she was talking on the phone.

'Mum, I don't think it is a good idea. I've already thanked him. He's too busy to answer unimportant telephone calls.' She bit her lip. 'I'm sorry, I didn't mean you're unimportant. It's a nice idea, but it's not necessary.'

Ryan was listening. He asked quietly.

'Problem? Is that man bothering your mother again?'

47

She shook her head. Putting her hand over the receiver, she explained.

'My mum wants to thank you and I'm trying to put her off.'

'I always enjoy talking to women when they're fighting for my attention.'

'It's a waste of your time.'

'Tut, tut! What a way to treat your mother! Put her through.'

He disappeared and Kate was speechless for a second before she did as he asked.

She tried to get on with her work, but her eye kept checking the red button on the intercom. What were they talking about for so long? Eventually the light went out. She was tempted to ask him, but she kept her curiosity under control.

It was close to lunchtime before Ryan reappeared and stood in front of her desk.

'Your mother sounds like a nice person.'

She looked up into his laughing grey eyes and swallowed hard.

'Yes, she is.'

He stuck his hand into his trouser pocket.

'She invited me to tea on Sunday.'

'She did what?' Kate lowered her voice. 'I'm sure you have something better and more interesting to do.'

'As a matter of fact, I haven't. I'm home this weekend for a change, and when she heard I love home-made cake, she asked what I'd like. She's promised to make a chocolate gateau with all the trimmings.'

Her cheeks burned.

'Ryan, you don't have to be polite.'

He eyed her carefully.

'You should know that I'm quite polite by nature — but I also never do anything I don't want to.'

Kate looked down and ruffled some papers.

'Well, if you're sure?'

'I'm sure, and I'm coming.' He looked at the wall clock. 'I just have time to get something to eat before I find out what that clothing manufacturer wants.'

She nodded.

With his coat flapping, he left.

* * *

Hugh kept her busy, finding information about a couple of prospective people he was interviewing for the job of organising a wedding for someone from the film industry.

'You can't just throw anyone into that shark tank,' he commented when she handed him the folder with the information. They need nerves of steel and armoured plating.

'I've seen some trained, professional organisers reduced to the state of a shivering jelly by people from the world of entertainment.

'The prospective bride or groom often have ridiculous demands and they change those demands every other day. He eyed her list. That one . . . ' he pointed . . . 'he fits the bill, but it's complicated because I think he's a former boyfriend of the bride. If that's true, there's a danger it will explode in my face because I suggested him. I'll have to sort that out beforehand.'

Kate laughed.

'I think I saw a film with a similar idea. In that case, it got complicated because the wedding organiser fell in love with the bridegroom.'

'Oh heavens! Don't make me nervous by telling me things like that! I think I'll take him off the list straight away. Whoever it is, they need to take punches, avoid emotional entanglement, and do a first-rate job.

'The wedding costs will probably be astronomical, but I'm not complaining, if I can find the right person we'll earn a darned good commission.'

⋆ ⋆ ⋆

Her mother looked forward to Sunday but Kate was less enthusiastic. In fact, she was nervous. In the office, their roles were clear, but they hadn't exchanged much personal information.

She knew very little about Ryan. She hoped it didn't end up as strained small talk.

He arrived on time, a fact that immediately endeared him to her mother. He parked his silver BMW in the driveway, extracted a bunch of flowers, and strode resolutely to the front door, where her mother already stood waiting.

Kate remained inside and gave him a faint smile when their eyes met. He handed her mother the flowers and she gestured him towards the living-room.

He made himself comfortable and the conversation remained common-place — the journey, the weather, the locality — until her mother disappeared into the kitchen to brew tea.

Sitting opposite him, Kate tried to feel less nervous and even managed to ask him where he lived, and how often he managed to be there.

He noticed her nervousness.

'I bought my own flat soon after I became a partner in the firm. In those days, the mortgage was reasonable and I'm glad I did it. My flat is now worth at least double what I paid for it, and I've repaid the loan. I now have more money in my pocket for other things.'

'Such as?'

'Theatre, holidays now and then, books, weekends exploring other parts of the country.'

'Do you have enough spare time? You seem to work hard, very hard, and spend a lot of time abroad.'

He shrugged.

'We all have to work for our money. I enjoy what I do. I'm hoping to reduce the amount of travelling I do in the near future. I now have numerous, regular clients in Europe, and they know I can find them the right recruit without long personal discussions beforehand.

'Hugh and I handle different areas, so we wouldn't clash on the domestic side of things either. I don't need to run after commissions in the way I did when I began.

'Once you've done a good job, people

remember you and come back whenever a new employee is wanted.'

Her mother reappeared and put cake, sandwiches and scones, and her best tea service on the table.

Ryan fondled the head of her mother's spaniel who had followed her mother back into the room.

'Do you like dogs, Mr Hayes? If not, I'll shut Jolly in the kitchen. He won't mind — he sleeps there anyway.'

'No problem. I like dogs. We used to have one when I was a kid. I'd like to have one now but being away so much makes that difficult. Please call me Ryan.'

'Help yourself to whatever you fancy.'

He did, and took some tiny triangles of cucumber sandwiches.

'This a luxury. Usually when I'm home, I often face an empty fridge. I fill the freezer whenever time allows, but you can't freeze everything.'

'So what do you eat?' Her mother poured his tea and handed him a cup.

'I usually pick up a takeaway on my

way home in the evening, if I haven't eaten during the day, or I'm not planning to go out.'

Kate's mother shook her head.

'You should eat proper meals regularly.' He laughed softly.

'You sound like my mother.'

Kate remained silent for most of the time. He chatted with her mother quite comfortably, and she realised it was because he was used to being with perfect strangers. When he looked at his watch an hour later, Kate was almost sorry he was ready to leave.

'Thanks you, Mrs Parker. It was all delicious and it was very kind of you to invite me.'

'You are welcome. Thank you that you got that awful man off our backs. I hope to see you again one day.'

He stood up.

'Who knows?'

When they walked with him into the hallway, her mother turned to Kate.

'Kate, can you take Jolly for a walk, please? I haven't been out with him since this morning.'

'Of course.' She grabbed an anorak and the dog's lead from the hallstand.

Ryan said goodbye to her mother and they left the house together. He looked down at Jolly.

'Where are you going?'

'There's a local park nearby. I may even go a bit further, up to the heath. He loves it up there.'

He flipped up the collar of his coat.

'I'll come with you.'

She was too surprised to say anything.

'I thought you wanted to go home, but if you don't have anything better to do, you're welcome.'

He nodded and the wind blew some strands of his hair astray. Kate had the urge to reach up and tame it.

'Let's go.' She knelt down and attached the lead to Jolly's harness, glad to avoid Ryan's eyes. Thrusting her one hand into her pocket she set off and he lessened his stride to match hers.

Unexpected Encounter

They reached the foot of the hill and the path climbed in a shallow curve. The track was hard-packed and although the route was clearly popular, there were few people in sight. Jolly pulled and panted. He was familiar with the surroundings and anxious to reach somewhere where Kate would free him.

Kate glanced across at Ryan. He asked about when and how her father died.

'Almost nine months ago. A heart attack. My mother hasn't adjusted properly yet. She tries not to show it, but I notice she sometimes finds it harder to focus on other people's conversation these days, because her thoughts are elsewhere. Memories, I expect.'

His expression showed genuine sympathy.

'Not surprising, is it? How long were they married?'

'Almost thirty years.'

'At least she has you, and she must be glad you're living at home at present.'

'Yes, I'm sure she is. As soon as I know she can manage, I'll start looking for my own place. I love her and she loves me, but I don't want to end up with us both being solely dependent on each other.'

He nodded in understanding.

'I've been independent too long,' Kate added. 'If I wasn't around all the time, I think she'd look for other activities to fill the time. If she could find work, it would help no end. It would help financially and make her more resourceful.

'She has some friends and belongs to a choir, but the day has twenty-four hours. She needs to occupy herself with something new.'

He nodded.

'It's a bit of a conundrum, isn't it?

You want to help and protect her, and she likes having you, but wants you to be independent. I understand why you think there's a danger you could end up clinging to each other. That wouldn't be good for either of you in the end.'

Kate knew he was being honest. He was quick-minded, and always considered any situation carefully before he commented. She relaxed in his company and she liked him. She felt she could say what she liked, even if he was her boss.

'Would you like me to see if there is something suitable in the field of library research she could do? The fact that she hasn't worked for a long time is a disadvantage, but some employers actually like having older people because they are often more reliable.'

'That's kind. I'd have to ask her first. She was fully qualified. She was working doing historical research, and she was planning to try to join a PhD programme, but then she married and eventually dropped out.'

The aroma of sunned grasses alongside the path drifted along with them. They'd reached the crest of the hill and Kate bent down to release Jolly. He raced off to investigate the immediate surroundings.

'Can she use a computer?'

'For general things like e-mail, online banking and so on.'

'That's good. Try to encourage her to try other programmes like Excel, or websites for searching professional information.'

She laughed softly and was glad she was independent of emotional involvement with Ryan. He made everything sound straightforward and simple.

He followed Jolly's progress as he zipped around.

'He seems to be enjoying himself.' He turned towards her. The laughter lines around his eyes deepened. 'So am I.'

'He thinks he's a terrific hunter but I've never seen him catch a thing, apart

60

from the occasional poor butterfly.'

'Would you like to come to my party next Saturday, if you're free?' he suddenly said, taking Kate by surprise.

'Hugh will be there,' he continued. 'It's quite casual — a mixture of family, friends, and a few business associates. I have to repay hospitality now and then.'

She played with the lead and it jangled.

'It sounds like you have enough people to invite, without me. I'm not a party person.'

He chuckled.

'If you come, you'll meet some new people. Perhaps you'll meet the man of your dreams.'

'I'm not looking.' She looked up and a warm glow flowed through her. 'To be honest, at present my work is a lot more interesting than the men I know.'

'Ouch! That hurts.'

She hurried to back-pedal.

'Oh, I didn't mean you. I mean boyfriends. You and Hugh are both interesting specimens, and you do such interesting work.'

There was a decided twinkle in his eyes.

'I'm glad you think so. Come on, say you'll come to the party.'

Still reluctant, she finally gave in and nodded.

'OK — and thank you for asking me.'

'I'm not an enthusiastic party animal, either,' he admitted, 'but I know it's important to meet new people, and face new situations.'

The wind played with her hair. He reached forward and tucked some behind her ear. Her reaction to his brief touch fired her imagination and she stared up at his face.

The following silence was broken when a good-looking man with light brown hair and dark eyes came towards them.

'Hi, Kate!'

Kate gave the new arrival a weak smile.

'Brian! What are you doing here? You were never one for much exercise.'

He eyed Ryan carefully.

'Tom Seton is playing football on the local pitch. I'm supporting him and hoping I can join them for a drink after the game.' His glance returned to the tall stranger at her side. 'Out with the dog, I see.'

She nodded and turned slightly.

'Brian, this is Ryan.'

Ryan nodded.

'Hi!'

Kate had the feeling that no other conversation would be forthcoming. She was right. The two men were concentrating on Kate. Her colour heightened.

'We were just about to go home again,' she said. Ryan's brows lifted questioningly. 'Jolly has had a good run.'

Brian looked in the direction of the dog and nodded.

'I must be off or I'll be late for the kickoff. Good to see you again, Kate. I'll be in touch. Bye, Ryan.' He turned and began to walk down the path.

When he looked back briefly a moment or two later, Kate had Jolly on the lead, and Ryan had tucked her arm through his elbow. Brian's brow wrinkled.

They began the gradual descent again.

'Someone special?' Ryan asked.

She took a deep breath.

'My ex-boyfriend.'

'Still carrying a torch for him?'

'No, no regrets,' Kate replied, tight-lipped. 'We were too different, wanted different things from life. I didn't realise it at the time, but I did when I stood back and considered everything.'

'Right.' On the way back to his car, he reminded her again. 'Don't forget to come to my party. I'll give you the details next week in the office.'

'Don't I get an ornamental invitation on vellum paper with your coat of arms in the corner?' she commented.

His smile deepened into laughter.

'If you want one, I'll send it, but I have the feeling it might end up in the wastepaper bin. It's not worth the bother!'

Kate thought it was time to disengage their arms, but didn't force it because his and hers were hooked firmly. He released her when they reached the driveway.

He got into his car and lifted his hand briefly before he drove off and disappeared from view.

The sitting-room curtains twitched and Kate prepared herself to deny any personal attachment, and cope with the possible outpouring of questions from her mother.

Ryan was a private person and Kate still didn't know much about him, but he was more sympathetic than she ever expected. She could understand that her mother might be curious.

Party Time

Kate found Ryan's flat without any difficulty. The area where he lived was upper class.

He greeted her warmly.

'Get yourself a drink. You can leave your coat over there, in the spare bedroom.' He smiled and nodded. She moved on quickly because he was busy greeting other newcomers.

She found the spacious living-room. A beautiful Georgian bookcase stood against one wall. Everywhere else, there were glimpses of modern designer furniture. The colour scheme was muted cream and white. The room was already crowded.

She took a glass of orange juice from a waiting tray on a side table and hoped it didn't contain any undetectable alcohol.

She tried to forget her irritation that

she had agreed to come at all. She stood near an open French window that led into the garden and felt out of place.

Looking outside, Kate noticed there were inviting chairs and tables dotted here and there. Some tables had lighted candles and there were solar-light torches stringing along the edges of a flower-bed towards a group of trees that marked the boundary at the end of the lawn. The night was mild, and filled with silver stars on a black velvet sky.

All the guests were well dressed in casual designer clothes and there wasn't a pair of jeans in sight. There was laughter in the air, jewellery flashed, and soft materials swished as people moved around.

She caught fragments of conversation about the latest play in London or New York. A pair nearby were questioning each other about whether they had plans to go to St Moritz this winter or Biarritz for the summer.

A familiar voice interrupted her musings.

'There you are! Ryan said you'd arrived, I've been looking for you, but in this crowd it's a job to find anyone.'

Glad to see at least one face she knew, Kate laughed softly and lifted her glass towards Hugh before she took a sip.

'Yes, it is crowded, isn't it?

Hugh was looking smarter than usual in a business suit and tie.

'You look very smart, Hugh,' she remarked. 'I don't think I've seen you in a suit before.'

He ran his finger under his collar.

'You haven't, and it doesn't happen often. I wouldn't bother tonight but Ryan insists in inviting too many upper-class clients among this lot. They expect it. I'm glad you've come.' He nodded to someone passing.

'Ryan has to show appreciation to some of his clients who use our agency. Luckily, not too often, and when he does, he includes some family and friends to make it worthwhile.' He grabbed the arm of someone who was just passing. 'Like this chap. This is Ryan's brother, Anthony.'

The man in question stopped in his tracks.

'Hi there, Hugh.' His glance took in Kate, and a welcoming smile spread across his face. 'Who's this?'

'This is Kate. She's our new secretary. A very efficient secretary, may I add.'

'Good heavens, things are looking up. If that's the case, I might visit your office more often. My dear Kate, you have extremely attractive eyes and wonderful hair.'

Kate coloured and smiled.

'Thank you, and be warned. If you come to our office, you can help with the filing. You are family, so there's no reason you shouldn't help out with mundane tasks.'

Hugh's eyes twinkled.

'I'd like to see Anthony doing that. He's a lawyer, and he has a cosy job in the city. I don't know what he does, but he has enough time left for enjoying himself and chasing women.'

'Look who's talking! You spend more time entertaining clients than working.'

'Entertaining clients is a very tiring job, my boy. Where's your mother?'

'Over there somewhere. I was just on my way to the kitchen to get some food then I intend to scarper. What about you, Kate,' he added, 'had anything to eat yet?'

She shook her head.

'Good, then come with me.'

Glad to be with someone who was friendly, she followed him. Weaving between people and pulling her along with him, he guided her into the white kitchen with its stainless steel equipment.

There was a buffet with all kinds of tempting food. Looking in Kate's direction, he nodded towards the food.

'Come on, help yourself. This is the best part of the whole evening.'

Smiling, she picked up a knife and

fork, put a selection of food on her plate, and began to eat some smoked salmon with a delicious rice salad.

'This is good.' Noting how quickly his food vanished, she smiled. 'Is that your lot, or are you going to reload?'

He brushed the corner of his mouth with his finger.

'Not much more. I'll finish off with something from the dessert section.'

She laughed as he moved further down the counter. Kate chose a portion of cheesecake and leaned against the counter, telling him about herself and learning about his loves and hates. For some unexplainable reason, they both avoided mentioning Ryan.

Ryan joined them a few minutes later.

'Ah, I see my little brother has been entertaining you,' he said to Kate. 'Good lad!'

'Hey less of that, if you please. I am only a year younger, and two inches taller. I also fancy her, so stand back, and watch an expert.'

Ryan laughed and Kate could tell they got on well. Ryan moved to Kate's side and threw his arm around her shoulders.

'She is much too decent to be wasted on you. She is the fairy godmother of our office. Without her, Hugh would revert to his old chaotic habits, and I'd have more work to do as well.'

Anthony eyed him shrewdly.

'Then hang on to her.'

'I intend to,' He reached down and kissed Kate's cheek.

She felt disorientated for a moment. Her throat was tight, and she hoped no-one else could hear how loudly her heart was thumping. She told herself to be sensible. How silly! It would be madness to end up infatuated with her boss.

'A fairy godmother is often plump and carries a magic wand.' She laughed. 'I am not plump and I don't have a magic wand. I wish that I did, then I'd grant all my own wishes. You should be sparing with your praises,

Ryan, otherwise I'll be asking for a wage increase.'

He eyed her carefully.

'I think you might even have a basis for discussion. Come and meet my mother, Hugh's sister. You've met the black sheep of the family.' He tilted his head in the direction of his brother and ducked as Anthony attempted a swipe.

Grabbing Kate's hand, Ryan dragged her towards the door. Kate looked back and shrugged at Anthony. He shrugged back and then concentrated on his mousse au chocolat.

His mother was standing on the side, talking to Hugh and another woman. She was a pleasant-looking middle-aged woman with a good figure and kind grey eyes which reminded Kate of Ryan's.

Kate straightened her dress and waited as Ryan introduced her. The room was a hub of conversation and laughter, and around them glasses tinkled and people bantered.

'So, you're Kate. I'm pleased to meet you.'

'I'm pleased to meet you, too.'

'Hugh has been telling me how you've restored order to that place. I haven't been there often, but the last time I called, on my way to the West End, it was an abysmal, untidy mess.'

Kate's gentle laugh rippled and her eyes twinkled.

'Yes, it was pretty awful, and needed straightening out, but I think we have it under control again now.'

Sally Hayes looked accusingly at her brother.

'I suppose I shouldn't be surprised any more. My brother has always been in the same state of confused disorder. It's not surprising his professional life is chaotic.'

Hugh took a sip of his drink.

'My professional life has always been under control,' he replied nonchalantly. 'You've always been over-scrupulous and too concerned with minor details. I won't be rude and add 'busybody', but you do concern yourself too much with other people's business.'

They eyed each other and began to laugh. Kate could tell they liked each other, even though they weren't blind to each other's shortcomings.

Ryan's mother focused her attention on her son, and the young woman at his side. If Hugh liked this girl, that was an accolade. She must get to know her better. Hugh didn't have time for social butterflies or women with empty brains. It was a pity she wasn't 30 years older.

As far as she knew, he'd never met anyone who'd bowled him over, even though he must have met thousands of women in the course of his life. Pity, because despite his weak points, he was a decent man.

Sally hoped that Ryan wouldn't end up like Hugh. He seemed to know countless women, and probably had affairs now and then but they had always been short-lived. Before she knew he was seeing someone regularly, it was usually almost over.

Apart from Geraldine, no-one had lasted very long — but Geraldine wasn't just intelligent and pretty, she was ambitious and unfortunately very materialistic, too. She dropped Ryan when she met another man who was richer and seemed to be doing better career-wise.

Sally noted how Ryan watched Kate. She was his colleague, but one never knew — she'd have to keep an eye on things.

'You must have a hard time putting up with these two. I'm surprised the agency hasn't gone bust before now. An office has to be organised and working efficiently.'

Ryan sighed.

'I am very organised and very professional. We have never been anywhere near bankruptcy. When I joined Hugh, the agency was already making a small profit.'

'You should have taught him to have more method in his madness after you became a partner.'

Ryan looked at Hugh and his mouth quirked.

'Impossible! No-one can do that. I'm glad we now have Kate, and that she manages to keep things under control.'

Hugh laughed and he viewed his nephew indulgently.

Sally Hayes looked around.

'Ryan, your father is over by the fireplace talking to Walter. Why don't you introduce Kate? I'm sure he'd like to meet the latest addition to your office.'

Ryan nodded, and Kate felt pleased as he turned towards her. A familiar voice interrupted them.

Alone in Paris

Louise was wearing a chiffon lace dress in pale blue and her hair was pinned in a complicated French pleat that left small tendrils of her blonde hair curling at the side of her face.

Kate couldn't help wondering if her own outfit stood comparison. She'd deliberated a long time on what to wear and chosen a sea-green flared linen skirt and short jacket with a pale yellow silk blouse.

Her choice was limited anyway. She didn't normally need many formal dresses. Weddings or similar celebrations were the usual reasons she bought something more stylish. Her mother had declared the two-piece was just right. She'd felt perfectly comfortable until Louise appeared, and began to wish she'd bought something new.

'Mrs Hayes, Hugh, Ryan . . . ' Louise

said sweetly. 'I haven't had a chance to say hello properly. It's a delightful party — especially as I already know so many people here!'

Mrs Hayes smiled at her.

'Hello. I remember meeting you at the theatre a couple of weeks ago. You were with Ryan.'

Louise's glance flitted over Kate, and satisfaction pursed her mouth.

'Yes, I'm Louise. It was a very special evening, wasn't it, Ryan?'

The question remained unanswered. Kate gripped her glass more tightly and waited.

Louise laid her manicured hand on Ryan's sleeve.

'You must come and meet my brother. I brought him along specially. You said we could bring anyone as a partner if we wanted to. It's about time you met each other.'

Was it Kate's imagination that Ryan's features tightened a little?

'Excuse me for a moment, Kate,' he said as Louise slipped her arm through his. Kate watched for a moment as they fought their way through the throng.

Kate looked down and took a hasty sip from her glass of orange juice. She wondered why she cared. Was it annoyance or even jealousy? She wished she knew him better. There was nothing wrong in that, was there?

Hugh and his sister exchanged looks as they watched Ryan and the girl leaving. Hugh tipped his chin in the direction of Kate's glass.

'Can I get you something else? What are you drinking?'

'Orange juice. No, I'm fine, thanks. I'll get a refill myself in a minute.'

'Orange juice? This is a party!'

'Hugh, I borrowed my mother's car today. I never drink and drive.'

'Quite right! Have you met my other son, Anthony?' Sally Hayes asked. 'He's here somewhere. He usually spots any single women instantly. I think he has inbuilt radar. He zeros in like a thirsty mosquito.'

Kate grinned.

'I've met him. He was in the kitchen the last time I saw him. He mentioned that he was leaving soon because he was meeting other friends this evening. He even invited me to go with him.'

Mrs Hayes gave a wry smile.

'I puzzle continually about him and how he got through his exams. He spent more time partying and painting the town red than studying.'

Hugh laughed.

'But he got through. Yes, your two boys are as different as chalk and cheese. Take heart, Sally! At least Anthony hasn't got a drama queen in tow.'

His sister raised her brows.

'Do you mean Louise? As far as I know, she isn't anyone special. Anyway, he's not a child any more. I don't agonise that Ryan will make the wrong choice. Anthony is more likely to do that'

'Well, Louise Thalmy is acting like Diana the huntress at the moment.'

Kate didn't think she should be

listening to family gossip. Hugh started chatting to the woman at Mrs Hayes' side.

'I'm going to get a refill.' She slipped into the crowd and decided that she'd stayed long enough. She passed Louise when she went to collect her coat. She was coming out of what Kate presumed was Ryan's bedroom and stuffing something into her bag.

She smirked at Kate.

'I forgot something, the last time I was here.'

Kate didn't comment and went on her way. The hallway was empty when she left. Perhaps it wasn't polite to leave without saying thanks and goodbye, but no-one would miss her. She was happier alone with her own thoughts.

Driving into the fading daylight, she still felt irritated when she recalled Ryan and Louise going off together and how she'd seen her coming out of Ryan's bedroom.

She decided that Ryan deserved someone better than Louise but they moved in the same circles, knew the same people, and had a similar lifestyle. Ryan and Louise probably had modern views about relationships. Kate wanted a love that lasted and stood the test of time.

Perhaps Ryan and Louise lived for the moment, and let the future take care of itself. Her grip tightened on the wheel and she concentrated on the road leading home.

★ ★ ★

Monday morning got off to a good start. There were no urgent messages, and when Hugh arrived earlier than expected, he only asked what time she'd left the party and if she'd enjoyed herself. She explained she thought it was better to vanish discretely than to interrupt the flow and say goodbye to everyone. He nodded.

'I can understand that.' He picked up her newspaper from the corner of her desk, fetched a mug of coffee, and wandered into his office.

Ryan was outwardly polite when he arrived, but his grey eyes were hard like shiny granite. She guessed he must be annoyed — perhaps because she'd left the party early.

'Thanks for inviting me. I enjoyed myself,' Kate hastened to say. There was a moment of silence.

'Did you?' he replied with heavy irony. 'Somehow, I got a different impression. When I returned you were gone.'

She flushed.

'Yes, I didn't intend to be rude or ungrateful. I didn't want you to think you had to entertain me. You had plenty of other guests and you know I'm not a party lover. I didn't interrupt your mother or Hugh to tell them I was leaving. I didn't think it would matter and no-one would miss me in that crowd.'

His voice sounded as uncaring as his expression was remote.

'Perhaps you're right. It doesn't matter.' He picked up his mail from where it was waiting on the corner of the desk. 'I'm off to Paris this afternoon. I'm taking a man for an interview for the post of tutor. One of the French ministers wants a teacher for his children. I had all the details but I left it at home when I packed, so I need to print out another one, please.'

'Of course.'

'Apart from that, you can concentrate on Hugh's work today,' he added with a thin smile.

Kate could tell he was annoyed with her. She didn't understand why. She hadn't been a guest of honour, or someone special. She was just a colleague.

'I'll bring it in a couple of minutes.'

'Don't bother. I'll pick it up on my way out.'

When he finally left, he picked up the sheet of paper without further comment. Kate's emotions were mixed as she watched him cross the room and

85

leave. Why had her leaving early bothered him so much?

* * *

Next morning, Kate was making coffee when the telephone rang. Slightly disconcerted, she listened to Ryan as he hurriedly explained.

'That chap wasn't at the airport!'

'The one you chose for the tutor job?'

'Yes, he phoned and said he'd fallen downstairs this morning and broken his leg. I need a fast replacement. Get in touch with the second on the list. You can get it from my desk computer. The password is TickyBoo99.'

'TickyBoo99?' She wanted to giggle and ask why, but she didn't.

'It's in the folder entitled 'Teachers'. His name is Gregory Wilson. Persuade him to come, and put him on the next available flight.'

She looked at the clock.

'Flights are usually booked up, and

it's a public holiday in two days' time.' Her mind raced. 'I'll try to sort something out,' she added. 'I'll phone you as soon as possible.'

Kate phoned the second man on the list and decided to be honest. He could figure out he wasn't first choice if the interview was this afternoon. He was so enthusiastic about getting the chance for such a plum job that he agreed straight away.

'Good. It is too late to try to get a flight ticket, but the Eurostar leaves regularly, and I'll get you on that as soon as I can. I'll phone back with the details as soon as they're settled. Mr Hayes will meet you at the Gare du Nord and take it from there.'

She rang Ryan and explained what she intended to do.

'OK — but make sure he gets here. In fact, come with him. Book tickets and let me know the arrival time.'

For a moment, she was lost for words.

'I don't see why I need to come,' she

pointed out. 'Surely he can get to St Pancras and on the right train on his own?'

'I don't want to take any chances.'

'My passport is at home.'

'Send a taxi and tell your mother to give it to the driver. Call me back when it's all arranged.'

Breathless, she gave up and phoned her mother.

'Pack me an overnight bag, Mum. I don't know if I will be back today or not. My passport is in the bedside table drawer.'

Kate organised the tickets, rang the prospective candidate again, and arranged to meet him at St Pancras in an hour and a half's time. They should arrive in Paris early afternoon.

She rang Ryan.

'Good, that sounds OK. I'll be at the Gare du Nord to meet you.'

Catching her breath, she informed Hugh.

'I hope it's worth all this panic. What about money? Have you got enough?'

He reached inside his jacket for his wallet.

She waved him aside.

'It's OK, Hugh. I don't need money. I have a credit card.'

'Keep a note of everything you spend on our behalf. Ryan is lucky that you are prepared to help. This sort of thing is not part of your job.'

The taxi driver arrived with her passport and small holdall. She still had plenty of time to get to the station, and she set off.

* * *

Kate leaned back into the comfortable upholstery and listened to Gregory Wilson's nervous chatter.

'I already worked as a private tutor to Lord Sugdon's children.' He shoved a lock of his blond hair off his forehead. Mr Hayes has a copy of his recommendation.'

She nodded and hoped he had his own copy with him.

'That sounds good.'

'My mother is French and my father English, so I'm fluent in both languages. I've an honours degree from Cambridge and I taught at a private boarding school for a couple of years. My main subjects were Latin and Greek, but I helped out in history and English literature if there was a bottleneck.'

He seemed too good to be true, and his manners were impeccable. She decided that Ryan's first choice must have been exceptional. Kate smiled at Gregory.

'That sounds perfect for the job. Do you have any hobbies?'

His eyes lit up.

'I volunteer to go on archaeological digs in the school holidays. I've been to Scotland, Greece, and Italy. It's quite fascinating — finding items that have been buried for two thousand years or more.'

'I can imagine.' As he went on to elaborate with details of his various expeditions, Kate wondered if that was why Ryan didn't have him top of his list. Perhaps he wasn't the kind of laid-back teacher that children loved, even though he was probably a meticulous, dependable one.

The French countryside caught Kate's attention as they journeyed on. She felt a twinge of excitement. She'd visited Paris before, with her friend Christine, and she'd loved it.

On arrival, they descended to the hustle and bustle of the platform. Kate looked around for the familiar figure and saw him quite easily because he was taller than most of the men. He waved and checked his watch.

When they met, Kate admired his stylish calf-length cashmere overcoat, white shirt, and blue tie. She wished she was wearing something smarter, but also reasoned she wasn't going on an interview and no-one would notice what she was wearing.

'Good, you made it.' He glanced at the leather holdall in Gregory's hand.

'Give that to Miss Parker. Take it to my hotel, Kate. Here's the address.' He handed Kate a slip of paper. 'You can leave it with the receptionist. Come on, Gregory, we'll probably have to wait for a taxi.'

Kate followed them for part of the way, until Ryan turned right and they left her standing. He hadn't bothered to greet her, tell her how to get to the hotel, or even asked if she had any money. She shrugged.

She made her way to a tourist information booth and then to a nearby office to exchange some money. She and Christine had used the Metro during their visit, and she purchased a ten-ticket carnet.

When she found the hotel he'd chosen, it was delightful. It was small, quiet and in a side street within walking distance of the Arc de Triomphe. In her less than perfect French, she explained that she was leaving the bag for Mr Ryan Hayes. She asked if he'd booked extra rooms. The receptionist nodded and answered in excellent English.

'Monsieur Hayes has reserved one room for another gentleman.'

Kate frowned, puzzled.

'Just the one?'

'Oui, Mademoiselle.'

Feeling disappointed, she nodded and smiled.

She considered trying to get a return journey via the Eurostar, but after weighing up the prospect of staying, or the hassle of going back to the station and hoping to get a ticket, she decided the idea of an afternoon in Paris was too attractive to hurry home like a scalded cat.

Ryan had given her no other orders, so she set off to find herself a hotel for the night and decided she'd try the hotel where she'd stayed with her friend last time she was in Paris. It was in a completely different arrondissement to where Ryan was staying so there was little chance of them meeting.

She went there via the Metro, and was pleased to discover she could have a small, pokey, but clean room under the eaves. It was close to Notre Dame, perfect for walking along the Seine nearby. She left her bag unpacked, looked out of the window across the roofs and chimneys of Paris, and sighed inwardly with delight.

She would catch a Eurostar tomorrow morning and be back in the office before lunchtime, but this afternoon was hers.

Outside, she remembered that the district was home to 20th-century writers like Hemmingway and Fitzgerald, and she understood why. There was an ambience and a special atmosphere full of expectancy and delight.

She walked past Notre Dame towards the Seine and strolled along, breathing in the freshness of the air and watching the traffic on the water. She turned inwards towards the Jardin du Luxembourg. It was a beautiful park, and today it was full of lovers, tourists and Parisians. She wandered the winding paths and sat for a while overlooking the pond.

The afternoon was mild and sunlight warmed her cheeks as she watched children playing with their boats, and parents watching over them carefully.

Feeling hungry, she found an attractive bistro, ordered the menu du jour, and a glass of red wine. The bistro was typically French and the food was typically delicious. The waiter flirted with her, in English, as he brought and removed the various dishes.

She banished thoughts of Ryan and the interview. She had his telephone number but didn't intend to call and ask how the interview had gone.

The sun was on the wane when she walked to the nearest Metro station and she was glad she was wearing low heels. It was busy with tourists and people heading home after work.

Before she went inside her hotel, she entered a nearby bar and asked for a coffee at the counter. It was full of students and foreign visitors, enjoying themselves. She laughingly refused an invitation to join some young Americans at one of the tables, finished her coffee, and left.

Before she finally went indoors, she returned to the banks of the Seine and watched illuminated boats taking visitors along the river. Kate had gone on one last time she was here. The streetlights were on everywhere now.

When she reached her room, she phoned her mother to assure her all was well. She then sat for a while at the open window with her arms wrapped around her knees, looking out over the roofs of Paris and thinking how much she'd enjoyed the afternoon.

She vowed to come back soon for a longer visit. Paris was such a special place — even if you were on your own.

★ ★ ★

When she reached the office next morning it almost midday. The early Eurostar trains had been fully booked so she had had to wait for a later one.

96

After a typical breakfast of milk coffee and croissant in a nearby bistro, she had passed the time in the station reading a book.

The outer office door was locked but she had a key. Once inside, she saw a small bundle of letters spread haphazardly on her desk. She took off her coat, switched on the light, filled the coffee machine, and went to work.

The Right One

Hugh strolled into the office early in the afternoon. His face brightened when he saw she was back again.

'How was Paris?' he asked, filling a mug with coffee. 'Ryan still there? Was the interview successful?'

'Paris was lovely. I don't know about the interview.'

'What do you mean? You were with him, weren't you?'

'Only as far as the Gard du Nord. He took over and they left. I don't know what happened after that.'

'Didn't you find out at dinner later on?'

'No, we were in different hotels. I found one of my own. There was no reason to contact him. He didn't need me so I enjoyed an afternoon in Paris and travelled back on the earliest possible Eurostar this morning.'

His brow wrinkled and he stared at her with slight astonishment.

'You had to find your own hotel? He didn't reserve a room for you? I don't understand.'

Kate smiled nonchalantly.

'Don't worry. I had a lovely afternoon in Paris, and my room was very good. I kept the bill.'

His voice was very critical.

'It's not fair and I'll tell him so. Don't forget to note everything — train fare, taxi, bus, Metro, hotel, and the meals.'

'My meal was just figures jotted on paper. I don't have it any more. I could have phoned Ryan in an emergency. I knew where he was.'

'He expects you to traipse off to Paris at the drop of a hat, and then just forgets all about you?'

'He's a businessman, Hugh. He has more important things on his mind than what his secretary does in his absence.'

'He's always been very work-orientated, but I didn't think he'd lost touch with reality. He shouldn't have left you high and dry like that. I think it is about time I had a word with him.'

Kate thought it was very kind of him to care but didn't want to fuss.

'Please don't! I'm a secretary and it's my job. I had a great afternoon.' She tried to distract him. 'Anything special happened here yesterday?'

'There are some messages on the answering machine, but I haven't listened to them. You know that I dislike the thing. I was out all afternoon, so there isn't much to report.'

Later that afternoon Hugh popped his head round the door.

'Ryan just phoned. He wanted to know if you were back and if you were all right. He forgot to reserve a room because of the last-minute panic, and didn't know how to contact you later. Your number had somehow disappeared from his phone's contacts list.

'He left a message on the answering machine in the hope I had some kind of address or number. I told him it shouldn't have happened in the first place.

'If he expects you to jump at his mere bidding, he is responsible for you. He agreed and said he felt dreadful about it.'

Kate shuffled some papers.

'Is he on his way back?'

'No, he's off to the south of France for a couple of days.'

Kate nodded. Antibes was in the south of France.

★ ★ ★

A call from Brian flummoxed her later that week. She recalled the last time they'd met. She'd been out with Jolly and Ryan. Strangely, Ryan's face was clearer in her mind than Brian's was, and she'd gone out with Brian for several weeks. She'd always felt there was nothing special in their relationship, and was relieved when they finally split up.

'I wondered if you'd like to go to the pictures one evening, or do something else if you like.'

She was silent for a moment.

'Have you forgotten that you told me we weren't suited? Why should we go out together again?'

'I wasn't reacting logically that day. I'd had a rough time at work and I overreacted. Seeing you the other day made me realise I'd been too hasty.'

She was lost for words. She didn't want him any more.

He hurried to fill the silence.

'We can meet up with the old crowd if you prefer and see how it goes. You still meet the others, don't you? I stayed away because I thought it might be uncomfortable for us both.'

Kate guessed that, at the time, he knew that most of the others were angry with him. They'd figured out that the fact that Kate lived with her mother was the reason he'd left.

If he was prepared to face them again, he must feel more for her than she'd believed. She just knew the past was the past, and that they'd both moved on.

'We're going to a place called the Green Bottle next Friday,' she said reluctantly. 'It's down by the river somewhere. I'm going with Christine. It's up to you.'

When she told her friend Christine about his call, Christine frowned.

'You should have told him to shove off. He'll think he's getting a second chance.'

Kate floundered.

'I won't encourage him — promise! I just couldn't be nasty enough to tell him not to come.' Kate admitted to herself that it had something to do with her new job. It wasn't a run-of-the-mill job. It was very interesting and no day was ever the same.

Hugh was kind and even though Ryan was more difficult and she hadn't figured him out yet, she still looked forward to every new day in Jackson & Hayes.

She didn't need Brian or anyone else to feel happy these days. She also realised there was always a danger of romanticising your boss if he was young, attractive, and single, but she had that under control.

Christine's voice brought her back to earth.

'Brian will never admit why he broke it off. Don't agree to any solo arrangements. Stick with the crowd. He's not good enough for you.'

Laughing, Kate threw an arm round her friend's shoulder.

'I have no intention of giving him the slightest attention. I just couldn't kick him in the face. I think Julie always fancied him, didn't she? We can push the two of them together, or at least try to lodge the suggestion in their minds.'

Christine giggled.

'They might even suit. We'll see how it goes on Friday, OK? We'll go there and come home together. It's my turn to drive so I won't be drinking. I'm taking a couple of the others home afterwards, and you'll be one of them.'

Kate laughed and her eyes sparkled.

'What would I do without you?'

'You'd manage, but Brian was a mistake. Someday, someone worthwhile will turn up.'

'We all hope we will find Mr Right, but it isn't easy these days.' Kate grimaced.

'You can say that again. All mine have been Mr Wrongs so far.' Christine laughed. 'Come on, we'll miss the start of the film if we don't hurry.'

★   ★   ★

Hugh looked slightly harassed when he arrived at the office the following morning. Kate was surprised.

'Morning, Hugh. Something wrong? You look worried.'

'Yes, I am. Not worried — anxious.'

'Really? Why? What about?'

'My sister is about to go shopping in the West End. She's decided to have lunch with me.'

'And that's a problem?'

Hugh ran his fingers through his hair.

'Sometimes! She wheedles information out of me, most of which, may I add, is stuff that I never intended her to know.'

'She's your sister and you're not a convicted criminal. Or do you have some dire secrets that no-one should know about?'

He rolled his eyes.

'She wants to know too much. She goes on and on about the state of my flat and wants to get me another cleaner. I don't want one. Gloria is fine. She keeps the place clean and tidy, leaves things where she finds them, and doesn't fuss.

'Sally tries to find out how much money I spend on entertaining other people and eating out. She insists I ought to spend more time at home doing useful things like puzzling or crosswords or watching TV.

'To be with her is an hour of purgatory, and I have to pay for the lunch every time, even though she is better off.'

Kate laughed.

'Oh, come on! I'm sure you're exaggerating. It's not like you to be flummoxed. Just tell her to mind her own business. Have you ever done that?'

He looked surprised.

'As a matter of fact, no, I haven't — not in so many words. She's older and she's always bossed me around. I squabbled with her when we were younger but at some stage I gave up trying.'

'There, then! She probably hasn't got out of the habit and thinks she has to protect you.'

'Protect me? Bah!' He looked at the wall clock. 'I wish someone would phone with an emergency situation so that I could get out of it. There's no point in trying to pretend I have an appointment, though — she can see right through me.'

'Oh, dear! I thought she seems to be

a nice person. You've got into the habit of letting her dominate you.'

He straightened.

'Perhaps you're right.'

Kate carried on with her work and as lunchtime approached, Mrs Hayes arrived, looking smart in a grey costume, pink blouse, and patent black high-heels.

She smiled as she crossed the room.

'Hello! How are you? I remember us talking at Ryan's party, but then you disappeared and didn't come back. When Ryan asked where you were, and found out you'd left, he seemed annoyed. I hope he didn't get shirty with you.'

'Morning, Mrs Hayes. I should have told someone I was going, but I didn't think it mattered and that anyone would notice. Parties are not my thing, and I didn't know anyone apart from Hugh and Ryan.'

'You met Anthony and I'm sure you would have got on with some of the others. Perhaps next time?'

Kate wondered if there would be a next time.

'Ryan has probably struck me off his list.'

'I don't think so. Ryan is determined and single-minded, but he's not unforgiving. From what I understand, he's very impressed with the way you've cleared up Hugh's chaos and organised the office.

'The day of the party, he mentioned that someone from a rival agency had pinched one of his best clients, perhaps that's why he was so touchy about you leaving.

'Ryan couldn't figure out how the other agency had managed to persuade his client to change over to them.'

'Yes, Hugh told me about that. Ryan is good at his job and he spends a lot of time researching and picking out the right candidates for the right job. There is an unwritten law that agencies don't try to pinch each other's clients once they are on their rival's books.'

She nodded.

'It must have bothered him a lot. Normally he never tells me about his work. 'Is Hugh ready?' She started to walk towards his door. 'If he can afford to spend so much money on prospective clients, he can afford to take his only sister out for a meal now and then.'

Kate tried to prepare the way.

'Well . . . Entertaining clients is part of his job. I'm sure he enjoys his lunchbreak with you, but business is business, and eating with family or friends is a very different matter.'

Mrs Hayes viewed her and then nodded.

'Yes, I can see that, but Hugh needs a steadying hand sometimes.'

Kate chuckled.

'I bet he sees it in a different light.'

'He does!' She walked to Hugh's door and opened it. 'Hugh, I'm waiting.'

'Just a moment, Sally, I must get this contract ready.'

Kate knew that there was no contract to get ready.

Mrs Hayes returned to Kate.

'Is Ryan in?'

'No, I think he's in Brighton. I'm not sure where he is, because he organises his own appointments. I just pass on any urgent messages or requests.'

She nodded.

'Ryan has always been independent. I think that the fact that Anthony was always getting into scrapes made Ryan think he had to cover up for him. It's left him with the feeling he has to be in control. It's the same with girlfriends. He probably expects too much of them but that will change when he meets the right one.'

'Miss Thalmy, perhaps?' Kate said innocently.

'No, I think she is too demanding and bossy for Ryan's taste. I also thought that when we met her at the theatre that evening. When I asked him about her, he just told me to mind my own business.

'He would have reacted quite differently if she had been someone special. Nevertheless, I suspect there might be someone new in the offing. I recognise the signs.'

Personally, Kate thought it was wrong for Mrs Hayes to interfere, but some mothers were like that. Her own mother worried constantly about her, although she tried not to show it and never interfered.

Hugh came out of his room, and his sister started to walk to the door. Hugh hurried to catch up with her.

A Kind Gesture

'Kate, your Mr Hayes is a lovely man. He gave me some good news this afternoon.'

Kate was still in the process of hanging her coat on the hallstand. Her mother hurried to be with her as she did so.

'What are you talking about, Mum?'

'Come into the kitchen. I've just taken a casserole out of the oven. We can eat and I'll tell you all about it.'

Kate followed her mother into the cosy kitchen and her mouth watered as she smelled the beef casserole, with chunky carrots, juicy onions and a bowl containing steaming potato dumplings. Once seated, her mother served them each a generous portion, and Mrs Parker began.

'He rang me.'

Relishing a piece of dumpling

drenched in thick gravy, Kate looked up in surprise.

'Did he? What for?'

'He asked me if I would like to volunteer to help out at a library. Apparently, he's found a college where some research librarians help students to research. He persuaded the administrators to allow me to join them so that I can find out if I can still work as a qualified research librarian. He said that if I polish up my old skills there, I'd have a much better chance of finding a paid job somewhere else.'

Kate's eyes widened.

'Gosh! That's good news. Just what you need. He didn't tell me he was trying to find something for you. You're not a beginner, Mum. You know how to use a computer. They may use specialised programmes or new methods these days, but you know the basics.'

Mrs Parker held her fork mid-air. She sounded excited and her eyes sparkled.

'I just hope I don't make a fool of myself.'

114

'Oh, Mum, don't be silly, of course you won't. It's a perfect chance for you to update your skills. I'm sure that you'll manage. It was good of Ryan to go to all that bother. I'll thank him next time I see him.'

'I thanked him, and I just sent him a thank-you letter in the post just now — as soon as I'd got over the shock. The job is from two till five,' she continued. 'By the afternoon I haven't much to do anyway, and if I take Jolly out for a walk before I leave, he'll manage OK until I get home again.'

'It sounds ideal.' Kate reached out and covered her mother's hand. 'It is just what you need, Mum.'

Mrs Parker nodded.

'I feel nervous, but in a way I'm actually looking forward to it. I used to love my work.'

They continued with their meal and Kate could tell how excited her mother was. Kate thought that it was exceedingly kind of Ryan to take so much trouble and she would tell him so next time she saw him.

She hesitated to call him straight away. He was entitled to his private life, and she was bound to see him in the office. He knew the right people, had the right connections and knew what he was looking for.

On reflection, she mused that he was a researcher himself. It was never easy for an agency to find exactly the perfect candidate. It must have taken a lot of persuasion to convince the people in charge at the library to allow a volunteer librarian.

Her mother interrupted her thoughts.

'I'm going to phone Marlene when we've finished here. She's been going on to me for years that it would do me good to get myself a job.'

Kate smiled.

'You do that. I'm sure she'll be pleased for you.' Marlene was one of her mother's best friends. She was divorced and worked in a local bookshop, three days a week.

Kate helped her mother to wash up

and clear the table. She left her talking to her friend on the telephone, and went upstairs to her own small sitting-room.

As she switched on the TV to listen to the news, her thoughts began to wander again.

Ryan's serious manner and thoughtful expression were what strangers noted. He wanted people to believe he was immovable and inflexible, but underneath he could be very kind.

He was helpful and caring. Her mother meant nothing to him, but he'd still gone to a lot of trouble to help her.

Kate liked him. She admitted that she'd grown to like him, despite the fact that he'd forgotten all about her in Paris. In fact, she liked him a great deal.

★ ★ ★

At the first opportunity, she went into Ryan's office.

'Thank you, Ryan!' He looked up and his eyes shattered her resolve to be

117

calm and collected. 'It's given my mother a new perspective and she's really excited.'

He leaned back into his chair and played with the pen in his hand.

'Oh, the library business, yes! I'm glad if she's happy with the idea. It was no big deal.

'I happen to know the chief librarian from my days as a student there, and when I explained she needed an up-to-date insight, he agreed straight away, especially as she's going to be there on a voluntary basis. He contacted me to give the go-ahead quite quickly, as soon as I'd spoken to your mother.'

Kate smiled.

'She's still afraid of getting in the way, and slowing someone's work down more than actually helping them, until she knows the ropes.'

He gave her a crooked smile.

'Well, it's a long time since she last worked. It's easy to imagine why she feels nervous.' His phone rang and he lifted his hand to indicate she should wait.

Kate looked out of the window.

'What? But Gerry . . . I thought you were happy for us to represent you! I have a firm that's looking for someone with just your qualifications. I was going to get in touch this afternoon.' There was another pause and Kate noticed his frustration.

'I had them in mind, too. Well, if that's how it is, there is nothing more to say. I'll take your name off our list.' He replaced the receiver.

'Trouble?'

'Exasperation — that's the second applicant I've lost recently. I was on the verge of placing him, and the annoying thing about it is, he's got the job with the firm I'd already chosen.' He glanced at the papers on his desk and forced his lips into a stiff smile. 'Anyway, I hope your mother likes it and that it leads to some other kind of job later.'

Kate could tell he was still thinking about the telephone call.

'We're both thankful. Do you want some coffee?'

He shook his head and met her eyes. A tumble of confused thoughts scrambled around in her brain. She wished she could help and remove the frown from his brow.

'Not at the moment, thanks.'

'I'll get back to my work, then.' She turned and left quickly and told herself that her reactions when she was with him were perfectly normal.

An unwelcome telephone call had cut short their conversation. It was good to be friends in a small office like this one, but she needed to guard her own thoughts and actions. An air of indifference was always safer.

★ ★ ★

Louise called personally again. She drifted into the office in a cloud of perfume.

'Is Ryan in?'

'Good morning,' Kate replied. 'No,

he isn't, I'm afraid.'

'Oh, that's a pity. Never mind. I'll wait. You don't object to me doing that, I hope?'

Kate hesitated and Louise swept past her towards his office.

Kate called after her.

'I don't know what time Ryan will be back. If it is something urgent, perhaps you should phone him?'

Louise turned and her voice was almost courteous, for a change.

'Oh well, I'll leave him a note. It's not important enough to bother him. It's just an invitation to a garden party in two weeks' time.' Her voice was heavy with sarcasm. 'I presume you'll see him again soon, won't you?'

Kate nodded, and Louise went through the door. She didn't quite close it, but Kate couldn't see if she was sitting at Ryan's desk or standing somewhere else. She heard the rustle of paper.

Kate shrugged. What harm could she do? Perhaps Ryan and Louise were casual friends or much more than that, but she definitely couldn't ask.

A few minutes later, Louise swept out again in the same cloud of perfume and throwing the end of her cashmere shawl elegantly over the shoulders of her knee-length white coat.

Later Hugh returned from interviewing an applicant for the position of chef at a newly opened restaurant. He hurried in and gave her a smile.

Kate stopped adding a column of figures.

'How did you get on?' she asked.

'I think he'll do. The owner of the restaurant said the chef under notice doesn't know a saucepan from a frying pan. Even the girl doing the washing-up knows more about cooking.

'The man I interviewed this morning trained at Leith's School of Food and Wine. He used up all his personal savings to get his diploma. Since then, he's been assistant chef in a well-known restaurant.'

'Sounds good.'

'Anything happened here, before I settle down with the paper, and a mug of coffee?'

'Louise Thalmy was here. She wanted to see Ryan. She left a note for him on his desk.'

His brows lifted.

'I thought Louise was past history,' he scratched his chin, 'but I lose touch sometimes. I think Sally mixes them up. She mentioned Louise, Susie — or was it Sharon?'

'Gosh, that sounds like Casanova,' she said softly.

'Oh, it's not that bad. Sometimes he has to contact someone because of business and Sally can't sort the personal from the professional ones. Apparently, the personal lot never last long these days. I think Sally wants to be a granny and things are not moving along fast enough, so she pounces on any kind of information.'

'Does she follow Anthony's life so closely?' Kate asked.

'Of course. She is an interfering old

meddler sometimes, and I've already told her that the volcano will explode one day, with dire consequences.'

'Does she work?'

'Doesn't need to. I think she is on a couple of charity committees, but they don't occupy her enough so she concerns herself with her 'boys' — only they aren't boys any more.'

'I imagine that Ryan doesn't let her tell him what he can do, or not do, or who is a suitable girlfriend or not.'

He shrugged.

'He doesn't, but she carries on and doesn't recognise the danger.'

'Has no-one ever told her to let them live their own lives?'

'I try. Bernard doesn't want to get involved. He gets on well with his sons, despite what Sally says or does.'

'Perhaps one of her friends should try?'

'Friends? Her friends are a bunch of cackling hens, who only care about clothes and gossip.'

She laughed.

'It sounds hopeless.'

'It is.' He moved to the coffee machine and poured himself a mug of steaming coffee. 'When I look at my sister, I know why I never married.'

She laughed.

'You're not too old, Hugh. Perhaps you'll still meet the woman of your dreams one day.'

'And ruin my life? No thanks! If anyone phones, I'm not in!'

★ ★ ★

A few days later, Hugh approached Kate's desk.

'You'll have to organise the annual do soon, Kate,' he stated calmly. 'People expect it.'

'Annual do? What annual do?' she asked.

'Oh it's nothing elaborate.' He stuck his hand in a pocket. 'We've been doing it for years, more or less ever since Ryan joined me. It started out as a small get-together for our important clients, but it grew and seems to get bigger every year. It is difficult to leave anyone out these days. People are so sensitive.'

Kate looked at him blankly.

'I haven't a clue how to organise anything like that.'

'Oh, no panic! Just drinks and nibbles — it's that kind of do.' He flapped his free hand. 'You'll manage!'

'Who organised it in the past?'

'Sally did. She's good at that sort of thing. We always had secretaries who insisted it wasn't part of their job, and Sally never minded doing it. Now that you are permanent, I imagine it's your baby, isn't it?'

Her gaze was steady, but her voice was terse.

'I suppose so, but I've never done anything like that. There are firms who organise such things,' she said hopefully.

He shook his head and his eyes twinkled.

'Too expensive. We keep it simple.

Sally seemed to enjoy organising it.' He ran his hand over his face. 'Tell you what. Phone Sally, find out what she did, and ask if she'll give you some tips. She'd love that.' He scribbled down a number, poured himself a mug of coffee, and disappeared into his room, leaving her feeling deserted and confused.

Kate did decide to phone Sally, and explain how Hugh had left things in her hands and she didn't have a clue where to start.

Mrs Hayes laughed softly.

'Typical Hugh. He insists everything is simple, as long as he doesn't need to get involved.' She sounded almost cheerful. 'Would you like me to help? It's not as bad as it sounds. You just need to find an available venue and organise some snacks. I usually looked for somewhere that catered food as well.

'It's just a get-together of business associates and a couple of their friends. There are no long-winded speeches or that sort of thing. How many are expected this year?'

'I don't know. I only just found out I had to do it. I'd be so grateful if you'd help. If I see what you have to do, and how, I may be able to manage on my own next time — if I'm still here.'

Sally sounded breezy.

'Glad to. First step is to get numbers from Hugh and Ryan. Ryan is organised. He usually has a list of names and addresses ready. Hugh isn't. You'll have to poke it out of him. If he doesn't react, let me know. Hugh needs persuading and bullying.'

Kate laughed.

'I can imagine.'

'Last year they had roughly one hundred and twenty names. Once you have a number, phone me and we'll make the next move.

'I'm already thinking about a delightful place I discovered by chance recently, where the gardens run down to the river. If the weather is good, it'd be perfect.

'They have a good chef I'm sure he

could present some appetising snacks. It will have to be on a Sunday. A lot of people don't have time in the week, and they need decent warning, so the sooner you get a list the better.'

Kate shrank inside at the prospect of getting a list from Hugh.

'Will do, Mrs Hayes, and thank you for helping.'

'Sally, my dear. Call me Sally. Perhaps we can look at that place together and see what you think about it? I'll find out if they've any Sundays free in the next month or so. I hope they're not booked up. I'll also look for an alternative, just in case.

'It usually runs from eleven until early afternoon, and is a casual affair. I think that's why it is so successful. People recognise each other after a year or two, and we just need to say nice things to any new faces.'

Kate relaxed a little. Mrs Hayes knew exactly what to do and enjoyed organising. Kate just needed to sort Hugh out. Ryan wasn't a problem.

★ ★ ★

It turned out to be one of those beautiful English Sundays. The weather was a drifting kind of gentleness, and the restaurant was a perfect choice. The owners had placed garden chairs and tables in suitable places in the long garden.

A couple of willow trees skirted the banks at the end. Some branches brushed the surface of the river, and sporadic breezes shook their fragile feather-like leaves.

Kate borrowed her mother's car to get there early, but Mrs Hayes was already inspecting and approving. She smiled when Kate came towards her.

'You look very pretty this morning, Kate. That summer dress is just right for today and the colour is lovely.'

Mrs Hayes wore an ankle-length linen skirt and a floral silk shirt-style blouse.

Kate smiled.

'Thank you, and if we are exchanging

compliments, you look very attractive, too.'

'We do our best, don't we? No matter how old we are.' She gestured towards the garden. 'Perfect, isn't it? I think Hugh and Ryan can be grateful.'

Kate nodded.

'Couldn't be better. Did your husband bring you? You're very early.'

'No, Anthony offered, as a matter of fact. My husband has to entertain some visiting bankers today and, as I don't have a car, I persuaded Anthony to get up early on Sunday for a change and bring me. He's over there stretched out on one of the loungers.'

Kate followed the direction of her eyes and saw him. He lifted his hand and she waved back.

'Can I do anything?' Kate offered.

Sally shook her head.

'The glasses are polished, and the snacks are waiting to be arranged on the table in the conservatory soon. The chef said it was better to have it there because of any insects buzzing around.

'Why don't you get yourself something to drink and say hello to Anthony? I'm just going to inspect everything and I'll then join you.'

'What about Hugh and Ryan? Are they here?'

'Ryan is on the way, he just telephoned. Heaven knows where Hugh is. I've given up trying to organise him. Surprisingly, he always turns up more or less on time.' She turned away briskly and disappeared into the darker room behind the sunlit conservatory.

Kate took up her suggestion, picked up a glass, and filled it with liquid from a jug of fruit juice. Cubes of ice tinkled on the inside of the jug. She headed towards Anthony. His smile widened the closer she came.

Immune to His Charms

Anthony patted the edge of his lounger.

'Good morning. You're the best thing that's happened so far today. You look like the epitome of a summer day. The colour suits you.'

Kate sat down on the edge. She had bought the dress especially for today.

'Thank you, kind sir! I didn't expect to see you here this morning.'

He grinned.

'Two reasons — one, to give my mother a lift, and secondly I thought it might be a chance to see you again.'

She laughed softly.

'You are an inveterate flatterer. You can't stop, can you?'

'No, especially when I mean what I say.' He looked at her glass. 'What are you drinking?'

'Fruit juice.'

He wrinkled his brow.

'I'm driving.'

She looked at his glass of beer. He nodded.

'Before you say anything, this is the nonalcoholic version. I never drink and drive either. I've seen the result in court too often. Perhaps I'll have a glass of wine when I get home.'

She nodded.

'If you want to go early, I'll take your mother home.'

He shook his head.

'Not necessary. Ryan will be here. I'll stay for as long as I can persuade you to keep me company.'

A shadow covered Anthony. Kate looked up to find Ryan towering over them. She coloured.

'Flirting again, Ant?'

Anthony shrugged.

'She deserves appropriate attention. She isn't weakening yet but I haven't given up hope.'

Ryan eyed her.

'He's not to be trusted!' he warned. 'Be careful.'

Kate's eyes twinkled.

'I am, and I don't believe anything he says.'

The corner of Ryan's mouth turned up and Anthony fell back into the cushions, pretending she'd struck him.

'She can see through you,' Ryan commented indulgently. 'I'd better go and find Mum and see if anyone else has arrived. Hugh hasn't yet, but that's not unusual.'

Kate got up to follow him. He shook his head, smiling.

'No, enjoy Anthony's company a little longer. Most of the people we've invited already know one another. You don't know any of them but I have to mingle from the word go.'

Kate nodded.

'If I can help, fetch me. I'm not very good at small talk, but I can at least talk about the company, and ask them questions.'

He nodded.

'That's fair enough. See you later.' He turned on his heel and went towards the restaurant.

Anthony noticed how her glance lingered on his departing figure and couldn't make up his mind if she was just a loyal employee, or if there was more to it than that.

★ ★ ★

Kate learned Anthony was going into practice with a good friend and had plans to concentrate on trading and shipping disputes. He might even find new clients, or indirect connections amongst the people present. Kate could see how important contacts were in all kinds of business.

It was an enjoyable couple of hours. Kate noticed a cluster of women seemed to be buzzing around Ryan all the time. She reminded herself it was natural. He was one of the hosts, attractive, successful, and single. She joined in, seeking for any forlorn-looking individual to talk to, until someone else turned up.

136

Ryan's mother clearly knew many of those present. She took over from Kate whenever Kate looked imploringly in her direction.

Hugh had turned up on time, and even Anthony joined to help with the entertaining too. He flirted with the women, and chatted to those men he knew well.

Kate noticed that Louise Thalmy and her father were present. She tried to ignore the fact that Louise tried to monopolise Ryan's company often. Their paths crossed when Kate was wandering among the guests.

Kate was prepared to be friendly and chat, but it proved unnecessary. Louise viewed her and then moved on quickly. Spoiled beyond redemption, she needed to be the centre of attention, didn't like women outside her circle, and acted like a diva wherever she happened to be.

As the afternoon drew on, the crowd began to thin out. Kate left the gathering and went down to the edge of the garden. She enjoyed the quietness and watched the river flowing swiftly onwards.

She jumped when she heard Ryan's voice over her shoulder.

'It's starting to clear. Some have already left. When that happens, others start to think about moving, too.'

She nodded.

'People enjoyed it.'

'I think so, too. A lot of people make contact with each other through meetings like this. That man over there, for instance.' He nodded in the direction of a dark-haired man on the edge of the gathering.

'He's head of a catering firm and the man he's talking to owns a couple of first-class restaurants, so they have common interests. They'll remember meeting each other here today, and they'll remember we are their common link, and recommend our firm to others — I hope.'

'Word of mouth recommendation is always the best.' She looked back to

where his mother was talking to a woman in a beautiful sari. Her husband had left her to talk to a group of investment bankers in the City. 'Your mother is very good at this sort of thing, isn't she?'

He glanced back for a moment.

'Yes. I think it's because my father's position in the bank automatically formed her to be a hostess, and to entertain. Anyway it's in her nature to organise, and help if she's asked.'

Kate laughed softly.

'Hugh calls her bossy, but I've found that she has a real talent for helping and organising. I think she knows everyone expects it of her.'

He tilted his head and smiled.

'You're probably right, but no-one forces her to do anything. She can say no. My parents understand each other so well, after being over thirty years together, and they still support each other in a very affectionate way. If she'd wanted to do something else, such as paid work, she would have

done so long ago.'

'Perhaps she hasn't thought about it for some time. I bet nobody has suggested it for a while, have they? You helped my mother find that voluntary job and she loves it. I doubt if she'd have done anything on her own. She needed a push and your help.'

The dark brows arched mischievously.

'How's she doing?'

'Fine, as far as I can tell. I think she enjoys being in the outside world and having something to occupy her mind.'

'Good.' He looked thoughtful. 'I'll mull over your idea — perhaps my mother would like a change. Who knows?'

'What did she do, before she gave up work?' Kate took a sip of her drink and waited. She noticed how much she just enjoyed being with him.

He shrugged.

'Office work, I think. I vaguely remember someone saying she was chief secretary in some City company or other.'

'Well, that sounds promising, although naturally she'd have trouble finding a topnotch position after such a long time. Office skills have changed completely, and she'd have to cope with a different routine.'

He shoved a branch of the willow tree that swished between them.

'She doesn't need the money, and there are lots of organisations who welcome regular voluntary help. I think that might suit her down to the ground.' He gave her a grin and her heart thumped. He was a very attractive man.

'You may have given us a great idea. If I handle it diplomatically, and get my father in on the plan, it might keep her out of our hair. I expect you've noticed that she still thinks Anthony and I are roughly five years old.'

She chuckled.

'That's because she has too much spare time on her hands.'

He viewed her for a moment, and then he bent forwards and kissed her on her cheek. Kate had the urge to reach up and touch the spot. She swallowed a lump in her throat.

'You are unique, Kate.'

She pulled herself together and managed to sound quite normal.

'I'm not. I just have my share of common sense and logic. I'd like to be more spontaneous, but I'm not. Anyway, I think that outsiders sometimes see solutions that the person concerned can't. I don't even know if it's what your mother would want, or if it would be right for her.'

His eyes twinkled.

'But it's worth a try. She's still young enough to do something new, and just imagine how it would save Anthony and me from continual hints about getting married and providing some grandchildren.'

She smiled back at him.

'Then I wish you luck.'

He turned and looked towards the restaurant.

'I'll need it. I'll talk it over with

142

Anthony first. If I get him in on the plan, it will be a lot easier. Anthony can wrap my mother around his finger.'

'Well, find some work that will suit her, and have it all wrapped up when you suggest it. Get your father on your side if you can. I like her and I think it would be good for her.'

'She likes you too, she told me so.'

Someone called to him.

'It looks like someone else is about to leave. I'd better say thanks to them for coming. How did you get here? Do you need a lift home?'

'I borrowed my mother's car.' He nodded, and Kate wished for a silly moment that she could pretend she needed a lift.

'Good! You've done your duty for today. Thank you for helping. If I don't see you later, enjoy the rest of the day. See you tomorrow.' An impatient voice caught his attention again, and with a last glance, he hurried back to the others.

Kate lingered for a while. Anthony

was nowhere in sight. Ryan was talking to a group of people and one dark-haired woman had her arm tucked possessively through his. She decided it was time to leave. She found his mother, and then Hugh, to say her goodbyes.

Driving home, she remembered how Ryan had spontaneously kissed her cheek and wished she understood him better.

Her mother was watching TV when she got home. Kate was glad to change into cotton jeans and a T-shirt and grab Jolly's lead to let some fresh wind drive silly thoughts out of her mind.

Good News

One evening the following week, Kate's mother looked excited when she arrived home. Kate could see she was in high spirits.

'Something special happened?' Kate asked.

Her mother sounded breathless and excited.

'They've offered me a part-time post,' she replied.

Kate viewed her happy face.

'Really? That's good. How did that come about?'

'One of the girls is taking leave for a year because she's expecting a baby in six weeks' time,' her mother explained. 'They have to keep her job open, but they need to fill the gap. They asked if I'd be interesting in working three days a week, afternoons.'

Kate hugged her.

'That's super, Mum! It shows that you've fitted back into your old job very well.'

'Yes, and it's ideal, too. Three afternoons a week. It couldn't be better.'

'Even if it is temporary, it means that you will be able to prove you've had recent experience next time you apply for a job somewhere else. Who knows, perhaps you'll be able to stay there.'

'I'm not counting my chickens. I like it there, I like the work, and I like the other workers. I am the oldest there, but they were all helpful from day one. I think I'd like to stay permanently, but they can't afford any extra full-time staff.' She smiled broadly. 'I expect the others probably consider me as a kind of mother figure.'

'They must like you, Mum, otherwise they wouldn't be helpful. Dad would have been so proud of you. After all, it's been a long time since you last worked on a regular basis. It probably wasn't easy for you to have enough courage to try. So much has changed, and things still keep on changing all the time.'

Kate propelled her in the direction of the kitchen.

'This calls for a celebration drink. Have we anything suitable in the fridge?'

Her mother's hands flew to her mouth.

'Oh, I haven't even started a meal. I was on the phone to tell Marlene and I forgot all about food.'

Kate laughed softly.

'Why don't you take Jolly for a walk? It will give you a chance to calm down. In the meantime, I'll make us something to eat, and we'll have a glass of wine with it. Half an hour?'

Mrs Parker smiled.

'That's a good idea. I feel so excited inside.'

'Off you go then.'

Kate was delighted for her. Her father's death had left her in a dark tunnel. It looked like she was beginning to see some light at the end of it.

'Aren't you going out this evening?' her mother asked as she clipped on Jolly's lead.

'No, tonight is free. I'm going to the book club tomorrow and to the pictures on Thursday, but nowhere tonight.'

'Good'. Her mother opened the door. Jolly didn't need extra bidding. When they left, Kate made her way to the kitchen to see what she'd get them for supper.

★ ★ ★

Kate stuck her head around the door and Ryan looked up. His desk was full of folders and papers.

'I don't want to disturb you, but I must tell you that they've offered my Mum a part-time, one-year contract.'

He gave her a slow smile.

'That's good news. She must have adjusted very well.'

Kate nodded.

'One of the other workers is taking maternity leave.'

148

He nodded.

'Perhaps it will lead to something more permanent for your mum.'

'She's quite happy. It's for three afternoons a week, so it fits perfectly. I think a full-time job might be too much at present.'

He leaned back into his chair.

'As a matter of fact, we have also taken up your suggestion about my mother having something to do outside the home.'

'Have you? Were you successful?'

He played with a fountain pen.

'Yes, I think she'll have a go. Anthony and I talked to my father about it, and he thought it was a good idea.' He smiled at her.

'He didn't say so in so many words, but I think he realises she needs something else to keep her busy these days. She probably drives him mad, talking about Anthony and me all the time.'

'What kind of job are you looking for?'

149

'I've already sorted it out and she's agreed to join them next week. She's going to spend four days a week as a kind of receptionist for a well-known charity. Most of the people working there are volunteers. They just get cash to cover their expenses.

'I doubt if she'll be satisfied sitting at a desk, waiting for unannounced visitors, for long. I think as soon as she's got used to the system, she'll be organising events, and helping with fundraising.'

Kate nodded.

'Much better than worrying about her sons, or not having something worthwhile to do. She is very good at organising. She gets things done and people appreciate it when she works for them. You need people who are determined and have definite ideas, and she's one of them.'

He laughed.

'You can say that again.' His eyes twinkled. 'We love her, but the urge to organise our lives grows year after year.'

He paused for a moment. 'So, both of us have succeeded in helping our mothers to find something new. In fact, we are doing what I said my mother shouldn't do — interfering!'

'Ah . . . but we are not interfering in their personal lives, are we? We're just trying to make their lives more colourful. We are just giving them a gentle push in the right direction. Would you like some coffee?'

He lifted a mug.

'Had some not so long ago. Perhaps later?' He indicated to the papers spread out on his desk. 'I have to sort this lot out before a meeting tomorrow morning.'

She nodded and closed the door behind her.

* * *

Kate was clearing her desk when he came out and stood for a moment. She looked up and noticed he was frowning.

151

'You don't look very happy. Something wrong?'

Ryan ran his hand down his face.

'Nothing special.' He indicated with his thumb in the direction of his office. 'I haven't finished as much as I intended to and had to leave some of it, until I get back. If I didn't have a previous appointment this evening, I'd put in a couple of extra hours, but a promise is a promise.'

She looked down and nodded at a pile of papers she'd gathered in one of the corners.

'Well, don't keep your girlfriend waiting,' she couldn't help herself remarking.

His brows lifted.

'Where did you get that idea?'

She shrugged.

'Oh, I just assumed that was what you meant.'

He shook his head.

'I've promised to attend an exhibition at a gallery in the West End. He's a modern artist who paints for money.

'I've known him for years, and he made me promise to come, otherwise I would give it a miss. He seems to measure his success according to how full the exhibition rooms are.

'The last time I spoke to him after seeing some of his pictures, I asked him outright why he thought anyone wanted to buy his stuff.' Her brows lifted, and he continued.

'Oh, he knows I've always been honest with him. I can afford to say what I like. When I look at some of his work, I think that a toddler could produce the same effect. All disjointed lines, and muddy colours.'

Kate's laugh tinkled.

'Really?'

His eyes twinkled.

'I'm surprised that he still insists on me coming to his latest presentations. He's well known these days. Not long ago he admitted to me that he longs to paint trees, mountains, skies, and people with real faces.

'He did that in the beginning when

153

we first met, but those canvases never sold. One visiting gallery owner picked up a canvas he'd been using to get rid of his surplus paint on and he began to rave. Since then he paints what they buy.'

Kate's eyes widened and then she began to chuckle.

'Edward said he didn't intend to end up as a starving artist in a garret, so he grabbed the chance and splashed his way to fame. He comforts his split conscience while painting pictures.

'Not many people know that he can paint in a very traditional way. He gave me one of his paintings a while back. I have it on the wall in the guest room. It's very colourful and I quite like it, but I wouldn't hang it in the living-room.

'I'm hoping that one day he'll be famous worldwide and then it will be worth a fortune.'

'He sounds like a very interesting man, and I feel rather sorry for him if he's been manoeuvred into a box where he has to pay more attention to commercialism than to his inner voice.

'Perhaps he should flood the market with as many as he can of the modern stuff, and make lots of money. Then he can retire for a while to paint the kind of canvasses he wants to.

'Gallery owners might even accept his different style if the paintings are good enough. Lots of artists do change their styles in the course of time, not radically, but they do change.'

'To be honest, he told me that's exactly what he's planning to do at present,' Ryan replied. 'He's already bought a small, dilapidated building halfway up a mountain in the Pyrenees. He's saving until he figures that he has enough in the bank to stay there for ten years.'

She tilted her head to the side.

'From the way you describe him, I don't think he'd last ten years halfway up a mountain. He's used to receiving adulation, and being the centre of attention. Could he cope with that sort of lifestyle?'

Ryan shrugged.

'I can't imagine him sticking it for ten years, either — for a couple of months perhaps, but perhaps I'm wrong. I, and two friends of mine, shared a flat with him when we were at university, and as far as I can remember he did his share of keeping the place halfway habitable, so he does know how to look after himself.' He paused for a moment. 'Are you doing anything special this evening? Come with me.'

Startled and excited by the suggestion, she sounded flustered.

'No, nothing special, but I'm not dressed for visiting art galleries.'

He looked at her.

'You look fine. You always do.'

She viewed his tailored business suit and wished she'd decided this morning to wear something smarter.

'It's not a formal do with diamonds flashing and designer clothes flooding the place. During past visits to the gallery, it was very relaxed, and it's quite likely you're dressed a lot smarter than many of the others who'll be there.

'Edward has a wide circle of friends and his agent invites anyone who he thinks might be a potential buyer.' He could tell she was still hesitating.

'I won't push you, but if you haven't anything planned, come. It would be nice to have someone with me I know for a change.'

A Night at the Exhibition

Kate wanted to go, and threw caution to the wind. It was a harmless invitation, and she admitted that she wanted to spend time with Ryan. She looked at his familiar face and nodded. His expression lightened.

'Good.'

'I'll phone my mother and tell her I'll be late. That's a disadvantage of living at home. If I had my own place, it wouldn't matter. If I don't turn up and she knows I don't have anything planned this evening, she'll worry.'

'Understandable. Perhaps you'll be able to think about moving out again, once she's established in her job at the library.'

'Perhaps.' She shut off her computer

and tidied the remnants of stuff into the desk drawer.

He watched with an amused expression.

'You're a very tidy person, aren't you? I know a couple of secretaries whose desk look like a bomb's hit them at the end of the day.'

'I like to leave with the impression that I have everything under control, even if I haven't.'

He looked towards Hugh's door.

'Where's Hugh? I haven't seen him all day.'

'He hasn't been in. He's gone to some country mansion today. Someone enquired about finding a new butler, and he said he'd like to take a look and have a chat, so that he gets an idea of what standard is expected.'

'It's more likely that he was glad to get out of town for a day and ingratiate himself with some landed gentry.'

She looked slightly taken aback.

'Hugh does a good job, Ryan. I'm sure he has his reasons, and his explanation is quite logical.'

He threw back his head and laughed. 'I can see that Hugh has a champion.' His expression grew more serious. 'I know that Hugh does a good job, Kate, and I know that he pulls his weight. He managed to keep this business above water before I joined it, and his connections are impeccable.

'His methods are special. I couldn't manage his clients in the same way,' Ryan continued. 'I'm too business-like and down to earth. I like Hugh and even if I am amazed that his seemingly disorganised methods work, I realise that they do work, and that he is a reliable partner.

'He's a walking encyclopaedia about people generally and he was a great support in the beginning, when I didn't think I would ever manage.'

'That's all right then. Give me five minutes to renew my lipstick.'

He looked down at the oblong shaped Swiss watch on his wrist with a wry expression.

'Five minutes? OK, I'll give you that.' He started to put on his coat, and Kate hurried to the washroom.

She didn't have enough time to do more that renew her lipstick and mascara, and drag a brush through her hair. Hurrying out, she found him holding the telephone receiver. She looked puzzled.

'Your mother?' he reminded her.

'Oh, yes. I almost forgot. Thanks!' Kate gave her a short explanation and was grateful that her mother didn't ask for details.

She followed him out and he politely opened the door to let her pass before he switched out the light, and locked the door behind them.

They fell into step and the roads were busy with people on their way home after work. They made their way to the nearest underground station and, not surprisingly, the Tube was packed.

There was no chance of them being able to chat, but Kate was content just to smile at him now and then.

161

Outside again, the air was fresh, but dark clouds speeding high above them were threatening rain.

'It's not far from here.' He looked briefly at her shoes. 'Luckily you're not wearing impossibly high heels.'

'I can't afford to wear impractical shoes in the office,' she remarked.

He held out his arm and she tucked her arm in his. He slackened his pace and they ambled comfortably until they reached a brightly lit gallery window display with a single painting on show.

Kate viewed the picture and they came to a standstill.

'Is it one by your friend?'

Ryan bent closer, looking for the signature.

'Yes. What do you think of it?'

'I see what you mean. The colours are pretty dreary, aren't they, and I can't pretend that I recognise anything in the composition, either.'

He laughed. They disengaged their arms, and Kate already missed his closeness. He was more sophisticated, and used to making himself agreeable to women. She cautioned herself to remember that. This was just a pleasant evening he'd offered her, spontaneously. It wasn't a proper date.

'They have bits and pieces to eat, and drinks, of course, so help yourself to whatever you like. We could have gone somewhere and had a snack first, but to be honest, I didn't think of it until now.'

'It's fine.'

He pushed the glass doors open. The hum of a gathering of people immediately engulfed them. Ryan took her coat and added it to a bundle already populating the coat hangers near the entrance. He placed his hand in the small of her back and propelled her into the melée.

He was clearly pushing her in a chosen direction and soon some of the people there began to acknowledge him. He didn't stop, just exchanged a word now and then, or raised his hand.

In Kate's opinion, most of the people

looked artificial. They gathered in little cliques, not interested in the world around them. She didn't say so to Ryan, because she presumed he felt at home amongst them.

Kate almost lost him as groups moved and jostled, so Ryan held her hand tighter and drew her along with him. Kate wondered if anyone actually looked at the paintings on the walls.

They came to a halt in one of the corners where some people were crowded around a youngish man. When he caught sight of Ryan, he came towards him.

He had curly hair, bright black eyes, and was wearing baggy trousers and some kind of khaki top that was so shabby it wouldn't have been on offer in a charity shop. He had a glass in one hand and slapped Ryan on his back with the other.

'You came then? It's good to see you. Terry is around somewhere. He came with his wife. Did you know that he's a banker? After I'd insulted his choice of profession a couple of times, he moved off.'

Ryan gave him a crooked smile.

Edward inspected the woman at his side.

'Who's this? I haven't missed something have I? You're not engaged, or married by any chance?'

'No, this is a very good friend. This is Kate.'

Edward nodded.

'Interesting bone structure, lovely eyes, gorgeous hair. Hi there, Kate! What are you doing wasting your time with this adventurer?'

'Just tagging along.'

He nodded and viewed her more carefully. He was about to say something when a blonde woman in a pale blue chiffon blouse and tailored black trousers interrupted them. She stuck her arms through Ryan's arm.

'Ryan, darling, I just spotted you. You must come and meet the crowd. We're over there in the corner. We haven't seen you for ages. Have you been hiding?' She gave Kate a fleeting glance. 'Or have you a plausible explanation?'

Ryan glanced at Kate. Kate wondered how to find a way of liberating him from the misguided assumption that he had to stay at her side. She smiled at Edward.

'Will you show me round your paintings? Ryan told me that you're a modern artist. I know nothing about art, so I'll be glad to hear all about it from the horse's mouth.'

Edward looked at her in surprise.

'You are the first person this evening who has mentioned my paintings, apart from my agent. He told me that we've sold a couple. Any chance of you buying one?'

She ignored the sight of the woman's guiding hand on Ryan's arm but couldn't help noticing that it took him a moment to respond. He looked at Kate and knitted his brow, before he finally decided to be polite.

'I'll be back, Kate, won't be long!' She nodded and hoped that he didn't feel responsible for her. She was old enough to take care of herself. He followed the woman with a fleeting backward look as she threaded her way to where she came from.

Kate turned her attention to Edward again. She unknotted the silk scarf around her throat, and shoved it in her shoulder bag.

'I could never afford one of your paintings. Ryan told me you are quite famous already.'

Edward looked at Ryan's head moving above the crowd as he made his way across the room.

'Did he? Ryan is popular, too popular for his own good sometimes. Some woman or other let him down years ago, did you know? Are you two hitched up?'

'No. I don't know much about his personal life, past or present. I just work in the same office. We're colleagues, and he brought me along this evening on impulse.'

'It is probably the reason why he

doesn't trust many people any more
— the trouble with the other woman.'

She nodded.

'You must be a very good friend of
his,' she remarked, 'otherwise he
wouldn't be here this evening. He's
very busy at the moment, but he said
that he'd promised to come, so he did
and even persuaded me to come too.'

'Then he has taste. You're different
from the usual women who populate
his leisure time, and he likes you. I can
tell that.

'He's one of my best friends and he
puts up with my differing views and
lifestyle and tries giving me sensible
advice, so are you and I one of a kind?'

She chuckled.

'No. I think you and I are very
different. I am a down-to-earth office
worker and you move around in an arty
world. Ryan and I work together, but
no more than that, if that's what you
mean.' She glanced around. 'Do you
have time to show me some of your
paintings?'

168

Kate reasoned that her pointed interest might flatter him. She didn't want to drag Ryan away from his acquaintances, and she guessed he might do that if he saw she was standing around, alone and bored.

She didn't know anyone else, and no-one in this crowd looked like they would make an effort to talk to someone they didn't know.

Edward smiled.

'Oh, all right, but we need something to drink first. By the way, you can be honest about the paintings. Ryan always is.'

Kate was already thinking about what to say that didn't sound too critical. She guessed that whatever he showed her would not be to her taste. They wandered along the walls on the edge of the gathering. Their way was remarkably clear, because most of the visitors were in bunches and groups populating the centre of the room.

Now and then, someone noticed

Edward and exchanged a sentence or two with him, but most of the time she could follow him docilely as they viewed the various canvasses. One or two already had a 'sold' label on them.

They weren't as bad as Kate had feared, but the colours were dreary. She listened to Edward's remarks about brush technique or approach. She was at a complete loss about whether or not they were worth displaying.

He looked across at her as they paused in front of a canvas that had chaotic diagonal stripes in grey and black and a big splodge of crimson in the centre.

Fat tears ran from the centre of the red blob, and ended at the lower edge. At least this one had a bit more colour but Kate sensed the moment-of-truth was coming.

'Well, what do you think?' he asked.

'I admit I don't understand the first thing about art but I presume a painting should generate some kind of reaction, but to be honest I don't understand what your paintings are trying to say.

'I'm sure someone who knows what they are talking about would respond quite differently.

'Perhaps you should ask people who are used to appreciating abstract art. Is that what a buyer is supposed to do, or do you have to supply some kind of clarification when they buy it? I expect they look wonderful on the wall of a room full of modern furniture.'

He indicated to the canvas on the wall.

'What do you see?'

She gave him a barely susceptible shrug.

'Bands of colour in grey and black, dominated by a splodge of bright red in the middle. I'm sure you were thinking of a theme or an idea when you painted it. Do I need to understand what it was?'

He threw back his head and laughed.

'No, not really. My paintings do have official titles, but I think the majority of people who buy one of my paintings do so because they think it will fit in with their décor and they are not particularly worried about wondering what I'm trying to say.

'Most of today's 'would-be artists' continue to use a kind of 'anti-art' form because that is what the art-world accepts.

'Creating traditional painting and sculpture means an artist is in danger of being ignored by the so-called art establishment.

'There are some traditional artists who've made it, despite all the hurdles. It's also a fact that many 'modern' artists haven't been adequately trained in the disciplines of drawing, painting or in sculpting — on which traditional art depends.

'Does an ordinary person view a picture and imagine that black squares on a white field could be interpreted as black being the artist's feelings and the white fields as the void beyond those feelings?'

'I imagine a lot of people, like me, wouldn't have the slightest idea what black, white, triangles, squiggles, lines, or such, would mean.

'Sorry, Edward, but I like to recognise what's painted. Andy Warhol is a modern artist, but I can at least recognise it's a tin of soup or Marilyn Monroe.'

'True, but remember that Warhol once explained that he didn't love roses, bottles, or the like and didn't want to paint them lovingly and patiently, he said he wanted to be a machine. He used something that was already there. Machines don't have intentions or emotions.

'Even if you recognise what's painted, the artist might still be expressing something you don't recognise. If you don't recognise what he's painted, it makes the whole thing a lot more complicated.'

She shrugged.

'I can tell I've a lot to learn.'

Edward laughed and threw his arm around her shoulder.

'You're OK. I like honest people. Let's view the rest and if you like one that hasn't been sold, I'll explain what it means and give it to you as a present.'

With his arm linked through hers, they wandered around the rest of the display. Kate caught Ryan's eyes once in a gap in the crowd. She lifted her hand to reassure him, and he nodded back before the gap closed again.

When she and Edward had completed the tour, the owner of the gallery joined them and grabbed Edward by his arm.

'Edward, you must come and talk to that chap over there with the ginger hair and glasses. He's an American with a gallery in New York and he says he might be interested in displaying some of your stuff.'

Edward looked at Kate. She hurried to reassure him.

'Carry on, I'm fine.' She lifted her glass.

With a look of slight frustration, Edward nodded and then moved off with the other man still chatting away and feeding him with other information.

Kate looked at her watch and was surprised to see the time. If she left now, she could catch a train and be home before it got too late. She hated travelling in half-empty coaches late at night. Sometimes there were dubious-looking fellow travellers.

She decided to try to gain Ryan's attention to tell him she was leaving. When she pushed her way through the throng and almost reached him, she could see how one of the women had her arm tucked through his and although he had his back to her, he seemed quite relaxed and comfortable. She decided not to interrupt.

She made her way to retrieve her coat, and passed Edward on the way out. He was still huddled together with the gallery owner and the ginger-headed man. He looked her way.

She smiled at him and pointed to her watch. He nodded and waved. She waved back and hurried out through the glass doors on to the empty pavement.

Goodnight Kiss

The pavement outside the gallery adjoined a busy main road. It was dark and the overhead lighting didn't provide much brightness. She'd barely covered half of the way when she heard footsteps pounding down the road. She turned to see who was running, and her heart skipped a beat when she realised it was Ryan. She came to an abrupt stop and he came alongside.

She avoided eye contact for a moment, and gave herself a few seconds to organise her thoughts. He was still breathing heavily.

'Ryan, what are you doing here? I hope you didn't leave on my account?'

'You came with me, and I'll make sure you get home safely.'

'That's good of you, but I'm a big girl, Ryan. I can take care of myself. I saw you were busy with your friends, so

I decided not to interrupt.' She shifted her shoulder bag. 'I don't want to keep you, you can go back. I'm perfectly OK. I'll catch the train home. At this time of night there's plenty of room.'

His voice was smooth and low.

'If it wasn't for Edward, I wouldn't have known you'd left.'

'It's not important, Ryan.'

He didn't speak for a moment.

'There's no point in going back to the gallery,' he suddenly said. 'Let's go for a meal instead.'

He took charge with quiet assurance and she didn't argue. She knew there was no point in entertaining romantic notions about Ryan, but she couldn't help feeling elated about being alone with him for a while.

'There's a small Italian restaurant just down the road. Let's go!' he urged.

There were some ornamental dark green bushes in containers each side of the restaurant doorway. He opened the door for her. The ceiling was low, there were only a few tables, and they were almost all occupied.

A waiter approached them and nodded.

'Good evening. A table for two?' He held out his hands for their coats.

'Yes.'

'Follow me,' he said, after hanging their coats on a nearby stand. 'You're lucky this evening. We're usually fully booked, but someone just cancelled.'

While passing a table with a pile of stacked menus, he picked up two and led them to a corner table. He pulled out a chair for Kate.

Once they were seated, he handed each of them a menu.

'What can I get you to drink?'

'What do you recommend?' Ryan asked. He looked at Kate. 'Red or white?'

'Red, please,' Kate replied. 'Not too dry.'

'Then I think we have just the thing. From the Toscana, fruity and full-bodied.'

The waiter returned with a bottle. He

started to pour a sample for Ryan to taste, but he gestured towards Kate.

'Let the lady decide.'

Kate took a sip and sighed with satisfaction.

'Just right for me but perhaps it's not to your taste. You try.'

Ryan held out his glass for a sample. He tried it and nodded to the waiter. He filled their glasses.

Ryan smiled at her.

'You're right. It's very good.'

She relaxed with a feeling she could be herself and say what she liked.

'I'll give you a chance to study the menu,' the waiter said. 'I'll be back for your order in a few minutes. This evening I can recommend our Pansotti alla Genovese and Sarda a bennacafico.' Ryan nodded and he left them.

There was a heavenly smell of fresh brewed coffee pervading the room. Kate leaned back into her chair and vowed to enjoy the evening without worrying about whether it was sensible to be with him like this. She leaned across the table.

'Do you understand what he recommended?'

Ryan laughed softly. His hands were gripping the menu tightly and Kate admired his long fingers and neat nails.

'I think the Sarda a bennacafico are stuffed sardines, and Pansotti alla Genovese is outsize ravioli.'

She nodded.

'You speak Italian as well as French?'

'No, not really. I've visited Italy very often though and you soon get used to interpreting menus.'

She put her menu aside.

'I'll try the Pansotti. It sounds good.'

'It probably is. What about an appetiser?'

'Not for me. I'd rather stick to the main course, but don't let me stop you.'

'Then I'll have a salad and chicken palatta.'

Irrationally, Kate was glad he'd lengthened their stay by ordering an appetiser. She could sip her wine while considering his features, chatting, and listening. She asked him about Italy and they were soon discussing the contrasting cultures of France and Italy.

'I like both countries very much,' he said, between forkfuls of his salad. 'I haven't been to Italy as often as I have to France, but who knows what the future will bring. Have you been to Italy?' He paused for a second.

'It's a pity that we didn't share the magic of Paris together because of my oversight recently.'

Kate coloured, but didn't comment. They discovered they had a lot in common. Even when their notions didn't match, they still ended up laughing and not arguing or protesting.

By the time the main course appeared, Kate felt extremely comfortable with him. He made her laugh when he told her about some embarrassing situations he'd experienced with clients, and how he'd wheedled his way out of them.

They both jested about Hugh's methods, and they talked about family and hobbies. They discovered that they both loved books. Kate belonged to a reading group although he didn't have time for that.

Her impression that Ryan was reserved and almost unfriendly had lessened with every passing hour. This evening confirmed her suspicion that underneath a brittle shell he was a very kind and agreeable person.

The scent of his aftershave wafted across the table. Her chest tightened and she felt warm inside. The candle-light threw shadows across his features. His eyes were bright and his smile was constant. Her answering smiles were, too.

Kate loved just listening and talking to him. Like everything else about the evening, the food was perfect. She didn't want it to end, and they both lingered over their wine.

The room emptied gradually, and she came down to earth when he glanced around with a laugh.

'We're the last ones here, and I think

the waiter is hoping he can close the place and go home.'

'Then we won't hold him up any longer. Thank you for a lovely meal, and a really nice evening.'

He grinned.

'You're welcome. It was good, wasn't it? We must do it again,' he added and her heart skipped a beat.

He paid the bill and gave a generous tip.

'We need a taxi.'

'Nessun problema, sir. I'll phone for one. It shouldn't take long at this time of day.'

The waiter helped Kate into her coat and they waited outside for the taxi. The evening was still mild and high above them clouds drifted and revealed an occasional star twinkling far away overhead in the endless space of the universe.

'As far as I can recall, this is the area where you live, isn't it?' she asked.

He shoved his hands into the pockets of his coat.

'You're right. It's about fifteen minutes in that direction on the edge of the West End.' He indicated with his chin.

'A taxi will be too expensive for the whole way, but it would help to get me to the station.' She looked at her watch.

They stood together in the semi-darkness. Some reflected light from a nearby window lit up his face, and his smile. She was very conscious of his tall, athletic physique. He shook his head.

'I want to know that you get home safely. At this time of day, the trains are half empty and not particularly friendly places to be. Anyway, a taxi will do the journey in half the time.'

Some headlights cut through the darkness and when the taxi came to a halt, he opened the door, gave the driver a couple of banknotes and Kate's address.

Before he handed her inside, he stared at her for a moment and her heart turned over in response. Gathering her into his arms, he held her gently and her mind reeled with confusion.

He bent his head and kissed her. It was a slow, thoughtful, and delicious kiss. It was also so unexpected that her senses reeled and she wanted the kiss to go on for ever.

The pleasure she felt inside radiated outward and she smiled with happiness. She had no time to do or say anything. He stepped back.

'Goodnight, Kate,' he said softly, before he put his hand in the small of her back and waited until she was inside the taxi.

He slammed the door and stood waiting as the taxi pulled away. Kate looked back at his silent figure still standing on the pavement. She watched him until the taxi had turned the corner and he was lost to sight. She ran her fingers over her lips.

Pensively she looked out into the darkness at the passing dark silhouettes of buildings, gardens and other structures, without seeing them.

Kate was astonished at the undeniable knowledge that she had fallen in love with Ryan Hayes, even though she'd no reason to believe he felt more than friendship for her.

She wondered why he'd just kissed her. It complicated everything.

Taking a deep breath, she reasoned it didn't mean a thing to him. Merely a final ending to an evening that they had both enjoyed — a spontaneous gesture that meant nothing special. But it meant everything to her.

Biting her lip, a warning voice whispered in her head that she shouldn't make a mountain out of a molehill.

Later, when she was in bed, looking up at the ceiling and finding sleep impossible, as much as she tried, Kate couldn't remember in detail exactly what they'd talked about all evening.

She did know that she'd never been out with another man who made her feel so comfortable, relaxed, and whose company felt so right. There was a sense of understanding that flowed between them. She decided that he trusted her.

Kate wondered if he related so much to other women as he had with her this evening, or if he'd done so merely because he knew she'd never abuse his trust. She struggled with confused thoughts, until tiredness finally won and she slept for a few hours.

Warning Bells

When Kate reached the office next morning, she was full of anticipation. How would he react? She was alone for a while, but that wasn't unusual. She started to open the post and glanced impatiently at the wall clock now and then.

She couldn't stop thinking about Ryan. It was crazy. Her heart felt lighter and she had the feeling nothing could go wrong with her day. She didn't want to think about possible complications.

She ignored the possibility of how hurt she'd feel if last evening was just a passing fancy. Even if he didn't love her, she couldn't stop loving him. It was too late for that now.

Hugh breezed in with his usual cheery expression.

'Morning. How are things?' He slapped his newspaper against his thigh and looked longingly towards the coffee machine.

Kate smiled easily.

'Everything is hunky-dory.' She handed him his post. 'No-one has phoned asking for you,' she added.

'Good, that's what I like to hear.' He took the letters. 'I'll check these after my coffee. As far as I remember I have no appointments today, so I may toddle off home early this afternoon.' He glanced in the direction of Ryan's room.

'As Ryan is already on his way to Edinburgh, it means you're going to have a quiet day.'

Kate looked down and shuffled some papers into a neat pile. Suddenly some pleasure had gone out of her day. She pulled herself together and nodded.

'When will he be back?'

Hugh shrugged.

'Haven't a clue. I don't know why he's gone there. He mentioned it yesterday afternoon, otherwise I wouldn't know about it. Luckily, you don't have much to do with him anyway. Didn't he tell you?'

'He forgot, I expect.' They'd talked for hours, but he hadn't mentioned he was going to Edinburgh this morning.

'It's good when I know where he is. Sometimes people phone with urgent requests and I can send him a text, if I think it's appropriate.'

Hugh went to the coffee machine and grabbed a mug. There was a biscuit tin on the side of the table, and his eyes lit up when he took a handful of chocolate cookies.

After he'd disappeared into his room, Kate ignored the work on her desk for a minute or two. She felt more than just a twinge of disappointment.

Was the fact that Ryan hadn't mentioned his trip to Edinburgh a warning sign? She began to realise that working in the same office could get very complicated.

Even though she loved him, she would never be happy with being a passing affair — like the kind of affairs his mother mentioned.

Her heart thumped uncomfortably, and she became increasingly uneasy. She had no reason to feel angry or cheated. She had no right to him.

She straightened and with quiet assurance tried to concentrate on the day's work. It had taken determination and skill to get the bookkeeping back into shape, but she'd managed it.

Entering pertinent information was now an easy routine. She could tell at a glance that the firm was doing well.

The morning passed and there was one phone call for Hugh. She had to persuade him to take it, but a few minutes later, he breezed out of his office, brushing crumbs from the front of his jacket.

'That was Thomas Wilcox. I'm meeting him in the Fox and Hounds. I expect he's looking for someone for one of his dutyfree shops at the airport. Last time I had to provide all kinds of written assurances that the woman was innocuous and a safe bet.'

She looked up.

'I expect there have to be all sorts of stringent security checks for people working in airports.'

Hugh nodded.

'You're right, of course, but it means extra work for me. Thomas doesn't want to run around getting all the red tape sorted out, so he comes to me.

'If anybody else calls, put them off until tomorrow or better still, the day after. Finish earlier and switch on the answering machine before you go.'

With Hugh out of the way, and most of the other jobs under control, Kate decided to put a couple of hours into sorting through the old filing cabinets and throwing out anything that was older than ten years.

Most things were stored on the computer, but they kept the bills, expense sheets and the rest filed away in their original paper form.

She went out for a salad from a nearby bar and took a lengthier lunch-break. She kept thinking about Ryan and then continued with sorting. Satisfied with her progress, she looked at her watch. She'd finish half an hour earlier, and be home in time to get the evening meal ready before her mother came home.

Kate put her coat on, leaned over her desk, and was about to switch the phone to the answering machine when it rang. She picked up the receiver.

'Jackson and Hayes, can I help you?'

There was a trace of laughter in his voice.

'I think so.'

She took a quick, sharp breath and steadied her thoughts.

'Ryan. Hugh told me you were in Edinburgh. Do you need something?'

He was clearly surprised.

'Didn't I tell you?' he asked.

'No,' she muttered hastily, 'but it doesn't matter.' His voice sent a ripple of awareness through her. She waited.

'I thought I did last night. I enjoyed myself very much.'

She was surprised how composed her voice sounded.

'Yes, so did I.'

'Someone has given me complimentary tickets for a new play in the West End on Thursday. I wondered if you'd like to come.'

She answered quickly and was glad that he couldn't see how the colour had flooded her cheeks.

'Yes, I'd like that.'

'Good. Six-thirty? I'll be back sometime on Thursday afternoon.'

Kate tried to sound natural, even though she worried that he could hear the loud beating of her heart.

'I'll meet you in the foyer,' she suggested. 'It will be easier that way.'

'That would be great. I wish I could be sure that I'd be there early enough for us to go for a drink beforehand but, at present, it looks like I'm going to be stuck here until the last minute.'

She managed to sound matter-of-fact.

'It's OK, Ryan. Don't worry. About

195

six? Which theatre?'

He told her and then asked her if Hugh was there.

'No, he went out to meet someone, and he wasn't intending to come back today.'

He chuckled.

'Typical! Leaving you to hold the fort.'

'He told me to go home early too. In fact I was just about to switch on the answering machine when you phoned,'

'Then I was lucky. See you on Thursday.'

'Yes, till Thursday. Bye!'

'Bye!'

She sat down on the chair and stared into thin air. Was it wise to go out with him? She hadn't stopped to think. Was there any point in going out socially with Ryan? He'd never said she was special or even that he just liked her.

Either he thought she was just another available opportunity, or he was just being sociable with a colleague because they got on well.

A close friendship would ultimately complicate life in the office. Not for him perhaps, but it would for her. She didn't intend to have an affair with her boss. She wanted more than that.

She shouldered her bag, checked the coffee machine and the lights were off, locked the door, and left.

On the way to the station, her thoughts were still in confusion and she wondered if she should have refused his invitation.

That evening her friend called unexpectedly for a chat. Kate told her about her uncertainties.

'Go! Why not?' Christine commented. 'There is nothing wrong with going out with him for the evening. I understand why you're worried — in case he's merely scheming — but just remember you can opt out any time you feel unhappy about it. You have nothing to lose. From what you told me about him, he doesn't seem to be that kind of man, but you never know!'

Fire of Passion

Kate took a lot of time choosing what to wear. In the end, she opted for a short summer dress with a matching linen jacket. It was smart but casual. People were already going inside when she reached the theatre.

She went into the busy foyer. Ryan was taller than most of the men there, so she saw him quite easily and made her way towards him. She felt a little nervous and he made her breathless for a second when they met.

He was deliciously attractive in a black jacket and jeans, a white shirt and a loosely knotted tie. He held her upper arm for a moment and smiled with satisfaction.

'You look perfect and you made it in plenty of time, that's good.'

'It wasn't so difficult for me. Did you have a good journey?'

'Landed roughly three hours ago.' He laughed softly. 'Just enough time to shower and change.' Kate could smell the tantalising sandalwood of his aftershave.

His hand captured hers possessively and she couldn't help thinking how warm and strong his hand was as he grasped hers.

'Let's find our seats.'

She considered how he completely captivated her without the slightest effort. He looked at her for a moment.

'Is something wrong?'

'No, of course not.'

'Good. Let's go then!' He held on to her hand until they found their row number and seats. She immediately missed the warmth of his hand when he let go.

Kate looked around, studying the theatre, and glanced at her programme. She was completely happy to be with Ryan despite her misgivings and she felt elated because they were sharing the evening.

When the lights dimmed, she tried to focus on the stage. The play was about a stranger coming to live in a small village on the coast of Ireland and the interchange between him and the community when he tried to transform the way people lived and acted. Kate stole furtive glances at Ryan now and then, so sometimes her concentration wavered.

Because they were on the edge of the row, they were able to leave quickly when the play ended and were outside before the rest of the crowd.

'Shall we find a pub for a nightcap?' he suggested. 'On the other hand, we could go back to my flat. It's not far from here and it will be a lot quieter. I'll drive you home later.'

He hailed a taxi and she realised he'd decided she wouldn't mind going home with him. Kate hoped she wasn't going to end up regretting the evening.

She loved him, but she wasn't crazy. Ryan was sophisticated, and more experienced. She had no time for further thought before a taxi drew alongside, and he opened the door.

When they arrived at his flat, she recalled the night of his party.

Tonight the rooms were empty and she could see how well he'd combined elegance and comfort. He mixed her a drink, pouring a soft drink for himself.

She lifted her glass and gestured towards his.

'Because of you driving?' she asked. He nodded. 'That's not fair.'

He grinned.

'The only alternative is for you to stay the night, but somehow I don't think you will.'

She took a hasty gulp and ignored his words.

'I like your flat. Did you use an interior designer?'

He dropped down beside her on the couch and slid his arm along the back of it, until it was behind her shoulders. Leisurely, he stretched his long legs.

'No, all my own ideas.'

'I should have known, shouldn't I? I like it.'

He chuckled and nodded.

'What did you think about the play?'

Kate relaxed.

'It was thought provoking.' His smile widened in approval and he then began to talk about a client he knew well in Ireland. His smile was infectious.

He was silent for a moment.

'Do you know that you are a special person?' he said, surprising her.

'Me?' she said, taken aback. 'I'm not. Or do you mean that because I sorted the mess in the office?'

His fingers curved under her chin, and she gazed at him.

'No, of course not. You're special because you're concerned about other people, and because you know what you want from life. You achieve things with quiet determination. I like that very much.'

Kate's mouth curved into a smile.

'All that applies to you, too. At first I thought you were unsympathetic.'

He grinned.

'But now I realise that wasn't the whole picture. I think you like to keep people guessing. You care about the things that matter, you care about your family and friends, and you are a good businessman.'

He threw back his head and laughed loudly. Then he suddenly grew serious and reached for her. Her body tingled as he drew her into his arms and his gaze searched her eyes, before he lowered his face and kissed her.

Kate was powerless to resist and was drifting along on a cloud of happiness. At first, his kiss was surprisingly gentle but when his lips recaptured hers, it was more demanding and Kate gave in to her own eager response.

He held her from him for a few seconds then he kissed the tip of her nose, her eyes, and finally he satisfyingly kissed her soft mouth again. Her heart was hammering foolishly.

He steadied, his hands slid down her arms, and he spoke softly.

'Let's just enjoy being together and getting to know each other better. I bet you're not someone who rushes into anything.'

She was surprised that he understood her feelings so well. Her emotions calmed a little. She nodded.

'I do like you, Ryan, and I'd like to know you better.'

There was a mischievous look in his eyes.

'You don't have to explain. I understand. We have all the time in the world.' He let her go and stood up. 'Oh, I almost forgot. Edward gave me a book for you. You impressed him.'

Kate was grateful that he had turned the conversation to normality.

'Impressed? Why?'

'He told me you were honest, and admitted that you knew nothing about modern art. I think the majority of women he knows tend to say what he expects them to.

'I know for a fact that he tells them a lot of nonsense sometimes, just for fun, and they swallow it all without blinking an eye.'

Her eyes were bright with merriment.

'If he does that, it's not fair.'

Leaving the room for a moment, he called back over his shoulder.

'All is fair in love and war.'

Kate had a few minutes to soothe her emotions properly. When he was close, her heart thumped erratically, and he kindled feelings of fire.

She knew that if he'd continued to kiss her, it would have set her senses reeling and resulted in a dizzying dismissal of clearheadedness.

He returned with a book and a package.

'These are for you. It's a book explaining modern art with lots of illustrations, and this is one of his paintings.'

'Good heavens!' She unwrapped the clumsily packed picture and discovered it was the one with the red blob. She brought up her hand to stifle her giggles, and he threw back his head and let out a peal of laughter.

He looked down at her.

'I know — but actually it's probably worth a lot of money.'

Her eyes were still bright.

'But where can I hang it? My mother would have a fit. I'll have to ignore it until I have a place of my own again, then I'll find it a suitable position. Give me his address, or his telephone number, so that I can thank him.'

He nodded.

She looked at her watch, and was grateful that the evening would end in real friendship. She would have qualms and doubts as soon as she got home, but she wouldn't have to make up her mind about how much she loved him. She was certain about that.

'I'm flying back to Edinburgh tomorrow morning. I'm still holding interviews, but they're the last ones. I'll definitely see you on Monday or Tuesday. I'll get my car keys and drive you home.'

She realised, with pleasure, he'd come back from Edinburgh just to go to the theatre with her.

'You don't have to, you know that.'
She got up.

He covered her mouth with his hand.
When he took it away, he gave her
another fleeting kiss. Kate coloured in
confusion and when he began to jangle
his keys, she joined him in the hallway.

In the car, they chatted about
Edward and his plans to follow his
dream. The journey was over too soon.

She picked up her bag and on
impulse, she reached across and kissed
him gently. His eyes gleamed in the
shadows and there was a mischievous
tone to his voice.

'You are being wanton.'

She laughed.

'Goodnight! Thank you for the
theatre, and for bringing me home.
Have a good journey and a successful
day tomorrow.' She got out and closed
the door. He lifted his hand and with a
final parting look, drove off back down
the driveway.

Kate stood for a moment. She faced

the problem of whether she could remain in her job if nothing came of this emotional involvement.

Shock Announcement

Kate was almost glad she didn't have to face Ryan next morning. It gave her time to think more rationally.

When she'd almost reached the office, she was surprised to meet Louise outside on the pavement. She wondered what she was doing here.

'Morning, Louise. You're an early bird. Can I help?' Kate looked for her keys in her bag.

Louise tossed her head arrogantly.

'I hoped to talk to Ryan, but the office is still closed.'

'He won't be in today. He's in Edinburgh. I'm not sure when he is due back.'

Her hand flew to her mouth.

'Oh yes, how silly, he did say he was going there. I'll phone him instead.' She fussed with her handbag. 'Oh, by the way — I'm giving you a piece of advice — don't count on Ryan's interest for long.'

Kate's eyes widened.

'Pardon? What are you talking about?'

'Tommy Wyemouth saw the two of you at the theatre last night.'

Kate stiffened.

'What has it got to do with you?'

Louise slowly patted her blonde hair.

'A lot, actually. I don't suppose that you know we are about to be engaged. We haven't set a date yet, but soon.'

The breath left Kate's lungs and she was glad to turn away and put the key in the lock.

'If you and Ryan are getting engaged, why would he take me to the theatre?'

Louise laughed softly.

'Because Ryan likes women, and he likes his freedom. I didn't think he would ever pop the question, knowing what he's like, but he did — probably because he realises I'm a free thinker about partnerships and marriage, too.

'I would never try to cramp his style, and he knows it. He'll always come back to me in the end.'

Kate was lost for words, but she had to try.

'What's the point in getting married if you intend to cheat on your partner?'

She giggled.

'Good heavens, aren't you naïve? No wonder Ryan thought you'd be easy prey. He's an attractive man — but I think you are out of your depth.'

Kate turned the key in the lock. She spoke without looking at Louise.

'Then thanks for the warning. It wasn't necessary.' She hurried inside and closed the door with her foot. She took a deep breath and ran upstairs.

Inside she dropped her bag. Her hand flew to her throat, and tears gathered at the back of her eyes. She was determined not to give in.

Was Ryan a womaniser? She couldn't believe it but Louise had talked about their impending engagement. She wouldn't have done so unless it was true, would she?

The kind of world Louise desired

was planets away from what Kate wanted from life.

She sat in her chair and her fingers lay tensed in her lap. A hot tear rolled down her face, and she had never been more grateful for the fact that she was alone in the office.

Finally, Kate decided she had to pull herself together. It wasn't the end of the world. There was no reason to have any regrets and there was no reason that she should feel guilty or sorry for herself. Life would have to go on without him.

Looking at the letters she'd picked up on the way, she straightened her shoulders and began to slit the envelopes.

Hugh breezed in mid-morning.

'I've just had a meeting with Williams,' he told her, after greeting her and pouring a coffee. 'I need a copy of their contract. He told me I'd given them special rates — three per cent instead of five. I don't like quibbling with clients, but he's trying it on, and I don't like it.

'I remember bringing the preliminary agreement back with me after we met last week, but I couldn't find it yesterday. You haven't seen it, have you?'

Eventually Kate found it, left on the window-sill that overlooked the back-yard. Hugh pounced on it when she held it aloft.

'Good girl!' He read the text and slapped the surface of his desk. 'I knew it! It's all here in black and white. He just hoped I wouldn't notice.' He gulped the remains of his coffee. 'I'll catch him at his office.'

Hugh was in too much of a hurry to notice that Kate was unusually quiet and withdrawn. Gripping the contract, he hurried off.

She didn't see anyone for the rest of the day. Apart from a couple of phone calls from prospective clients, she was alone with her thoughts.

As time passed, she began to realise she was not just miserable, she was getting angry. Angry with him, angry

213

with herself, and angry about the way Louise had enlightened her.

Her mother noticed she was quiet and very pale, and asked if something was wrong. Kate managed to divert any other questions by saying she had a bad headache and wasn't very hungry. She escaped to her room and lay on her bed thinking of what to do next.

The next day or two gave her a chance to get used to the situation and strengthen her determination. Ryan said he'd return at the beginning of the week, and when she made her way to the office, she was nervous but resolute.

Climbing the stairs, she straightened her shoulders and went in. She was surprised to hear Ryan and Hugh's agitated voices.

Neither of them usually arrived before her. She went to Ryan's room and clasped the doorframe. Her heart tricked her intentions and skipped a beat when she looked at Ryan. His expression told her something was wrong.

'Good morning. What's up?'

They both looked up. Hugh hurried to explain.

'Ryan lost another of his best applicants to one of our rivals.'

Ryan's lips were a thin line and his eyes were angry. He ran his hand through his hair.

'I can't believe it. Another one gone! I worked for three days trying to persuade the Irish firm that I had just the chap they needed. I finally persuaded them to give him an interview.

'When I phoned him to give him the details, he told me that our rivals promised him they'd get him a suitable job fast, and as he was fed-up with waiting for me, he agreed.

'The really annoying part is that he was given the job I had my eye on for him, in exactly the same company. It isn't the first time this has happened. I've lost a couple of contracts in exactly the same way lately.'

'Wow! Can another agency do that? I also presumed you have a binding

215

agreement with your candidates.'

Ryan shook his head impatiently.

'We can't lock our candidates up and insist they remain exclusively ours. That wouldn't be fair on them or us. If they were just ours, we'd be obliged to find them work, and they wouldn't be able to accept a job somewhere else.

'We list all the details of our candidates if they are worth representing. Sometimes we're lucky and place them easily and fast sometimes they find their own job, and sometimes it takes a while to find something suitable.'

Hugh frowned at his nephew.

'This means someone has access to your information, and as you believe it hasn't happened for the first time, I can understand why you asked me to come in early. How can anyone get at your details?'

'That's what I'm wondering too. When I'm out of the office, I have my laptop with me all the time. No-one else ever uses it and in any case, they'd need to know my password just to start the thing.'

'You store information on your office computer too, don't you?'

'Yes, I transfer information back and forth.'

Kate paused for a moment.

'Do you ever print out details?'

He considered carefully.

'I suppose I do, now and then, when I'm working on an offer.'

'And what do you do with that list when you've finished with it?'

'I rip it up and throw it in the bin.'

'Are you sure you rip it up, every single time?'

He nodded.

'Anyway, no-one else would have access to my office. Hugh and you are the only other people with a key.'

Hugh looked at him.

'I may be scatter-brained sometimes about some things, but I am careful with the keys. I have the office keys on the same ring as the ones for my flat.'

Ryan looked at Kate.

'And you?'

'I have my set of keys in my handbag, and there are spares in the top drawer of my desk.' She crossed and pulled the drawer open. She held the keys aloft. 'They're here.'

Ryan looked enraged.

'I don't understand it at all. If someone is pinching names and information, the only reason could be to make money on it. If rival agencies get hold of the details, it is easy work for them, and they might be prepared to pay for them. Hugh and I would have no advantage, so that cuts us out.'

It took a second or two, and his questioning look, before Kate flushed bright red.

'Ryan, you are not suggesting I have something to do with it, are you?'

Hugh began to bluster.

'Good heavens, Kate, of course not. Not for a single moment.'

Ryan was concentrated on searching, his expression hidden.

'I was working on a print-out here,

some weeks ago,' he said tersely, 'and it had a couple of these nicked names on it. I can't remember what I did with it. I may have taken it with me and destroyed it later, or I may have possibly left it here.'

Kate noticed that he hadn't cleared her from the list of immediate culprits. His recollection that he may have left the list in the office didn't help one bit.

She crossed her arms in a defensive manner. Her expression grew hard and resentful and the feeling of hurt turned into white-hot anger. Damaged pride kept her from arguing and commenting.

No other comments came from Ryan and Hugh looked uncomfortable. She knew Hugh didn't doubt her but it looked like Ryan wasn't sure. All her beliefs of his fun, kindness, fair-mindedness and intellect faded away.

Did he think she'd sell information to a rival? Did he think she was a thief? She turned on her heel and tried to contain her anger.

Ryan ruffled through some thick folders piled on the side of his desk, and opened and shut drawers to check in them too.

Hugh followed her quickly.

'Don't worry,' he said firmly. 'We'll try to find the culprit, and even if we don't it isn't the end of the world. We'll just have to be more careful in future.

'I think Ryan is especially mad because it happened to him. Trustworthiness means a great deal to him. It's part of his character. It's not just the loss of a couple of commissions.'

Kate nodded to pacify him and looked down. She had no bone to pick with Hugh. Hugh trusted her, Ryan didn't.

She hung up her coat and went to fill the coffee machine as if it were any other morning. When she returned with the jug of water, Ryan was going out of the door.

Hugh looked slightly dazed.

'He's off to talk to the former candidates who switched sides,' he said.

'He hopes they can tell him where the rival agency got their names. The agencies themselves won't give him that kind of information, but the clients may have unknowingly picked up hints or even a name.'

She shrugged and switched on the computer. She told herself she was glad that he'd left. It gave her some breathing space. Hugh glanced at the wall clock.

'Good heavens! I promised to meet Walter at ten and he's on the other side of London.' He grabbed the phone and dialled. 'Walter? Hugh here, I'm on my way, something held me up. Get yourself something to eat and wait.'

After Hugh left, the office was silent again. She sipped a mug of coffee and wondered if it was just fate. She fell in love with Ryan, found out by chance that he was intending to marry Louise, and now there was his lack of trust this morning.

She loved him but he would soon officially belong to someone else and she couldn't possibly stay where her honesty was in doubt.

As the day drew on, neither Hugh nor Ryan returned or phoned. Just coping with the routine work kept her busy but she decided she had to do something to solve her problems.

Kate gradually concluded she had to leave. It would solve both the problem of having to see Ryan every day, and would leave the company free to find someone else. Someone Ryan could trust.

It might look like an admission of guilt at first. She'd take that chance, just to get away. Ryan would be determined to find the culprit, and then any suspicion would disappear — but it would be too late.

Hugh wouldn't like having to find another secretary again but it was a way out of a situation that had become unbearable for her.

She'd have to find a new job, but that was better than living with heartbreak. She'd hoped they were growing closer, but perhaps he'd had other motives from the beginning. He'd never trust her fully again with any of his office work if he believed she was capable of thieving information.

Kate typed quickly and after reading it through once, she printed out two copies, signed them and put one each on Hugh and Ryan's desk.

'Dear Mr Hayes and Mr Jackson, I regret to inform you that I am resigning from my position here immediately. Today will be my final day. All my work is up to date.

'I realise this will be an unexpected development, but I find it impossible to remain, as there seem to be misgivings about my honesty. As you are an employment agency, I'm sure you will have no difficulty in finding a replacement.

'Thank you for the opportunities this company has provided me. Working here for the last couple of months has been instrumental in increasing my working knowledge and experience.

'I will never forget any kindness shown and I will miss both the clients and the company.

'I hope my resignation will not cause you too much inconvenience. If necessary, I can be available for phone and e-mail enquiries to help my replacement for a limited transition period as from tomorrow.

'I will not trouble you for a recommendation unless it is required. I hope if it is necessary that you will testify favourably on the work I accomplished.

'Sincerely, Kate Parker.'

She hurried, put on her coat, turned on the answering machine, looked around for the last time, and clattered down the stairs into the fresh air. She held back the tears forming at the back of her eyes and wondered what her mother would say when she told her.

She was sure of one thing — when she explained why she'd resigned, her mother would be on her side. She had to find a new job, but staying with Ryan and Hugh in that office was an impossibility.

Walking towards the station, she took a shortcut down a side street and noticed a sign in the window of a small bistro: 'Waitress wanted — four hours afternoons, including Saturday.'

On impulse, she went inside and applied. The middle-aged woman behind the counter eyed her carefully and asked if she had any experience. Kate said yes. She crossed her fingers, because she'd only helped in a local café to earn some pocket money when in the sixth form. The woman nodded.

'When can you start?'

'Tomorrow?'

'Right, we'll give it a try and see how you get on.'

Her conviction strengthened. Continuing on her way, Kate reasoned that it was sensible to earn a little money than nothing at all.

No Going Back

If her mother was bowled over, she didn't show it. She exclaimed that she didn't understand that anyone could imagine that Kate would steal information.

'You said that Hugh was on your side. You should have waited and talked it through with him, but I do understand you. I am surprised that Ryan seems to be the fly in the ointment.

'He seemed to be a very nice and helpful person. I wouldn't have my job if it hadn't been for him.'

Kate couldn't explain that she was leaving not only because of the lack of trust, but also because she loved Ryan and they had no future together. She shrugged.

'Something else will turn up, I'm sure. I couldn't stay there under the circumstances. The uncertainty about what Ryan was thinking about me when he was in the office would make every day wretched for me.'

Her mother patted her hand.

'You're right, I'm sure. We'll manage.'

'I'll start looking for something suitable tomorrow morning.' She told her about the job in the café.

Mrs Parker laughed.

'Trust you! Perhaps you'll find work as an accountant this time. I hope so.'

Kate managed a tremulous smile.

'If not, I can always look for general office work.'

They cleared away the meal together and then went to watch a TV historical drama in the main living-room. If someone asked her next morning what it was about, she couldn't have recounted much.

Kate stayed with her mother, not because she was particularly interested in the programme, but because Kate guessed that her mother would feel more at ease and less worried. She was glad when she could say goodnight and slip away to her own room.

Her throat ached and the anguish returned. Without any more distractions or interruptions, she now looked back on what today had brought, and a feeling of bitterness, loss, and utter misery overcame her.

She'd loved her job, she'd liked Hugh, and she'd found the man of her dreams. She'd fallen in love with the wrong man. She ached with an inner pain and knew it would not be any better tomorrow, next week, or next year.

Refreshing sleep evaded her. Only a sense of exhaustion allowed her to slumber now and then for a while, as she lay waiting for dawn to break on another day. She was glad she'd found herself something to occupy her afternoons.

★　★　★

Pretending to be more cheerful, she finished dressing and had breakfast.

Her mother went out to the local supermarket. Kate grabbed Jolly's lead and went with him for a ramble on the common.

Once there, she recalled the time she'd been there with Ryan, and wondered when, if ever, she would completely forget him.

After she arrived at the bistro that afternoon, she found that she was taking over from Cynthia.

Cynthia came from Ghana. She had a wonderful smile and an Afro hairstyle that she explained had taken four hours to create.

She was married to Charles and she had three small children and wanted to be home and have a meal ready and waiting when they came from school, or in Charlie's case, from work.

Cynthia supplied all this information while tying an ankle-length maroon apron around Kate's waist. The woman behind the counter nodded and smiled. Clearly, Cynthia was a chatty, friendly waitress. She contributed greatly to the ambience of the bistro.

After Cynthia left, Kate soon got into the swing of serving and clearing the handful of tables.

Most of the customers seemed regulars, and there was only a limited choice of sandwiches and cake, so Kate didn't have much difficulty remembering what everyone wanted.

She helped behind the counter too, filling the dishwasher, tidying up, or refilling sandwiches and cakes in the glass display case.

They closed at six-thirty. Kate wiped over the surfaces of the tables and stacked the chairs on top of them, so that the cleaner had an easier job of making things spick and span before the bistro opened again next morning. Her new boss gave her a slow smile of approval, and told her to go home.

The journey home was quieter than usual. Nearly all office workers had already gone home. Her feet were aching, because she'd been busy all afternoon, but she was glad she didn't have much spare time to think about Ryan.

Once or twice, she spotted a tall, dark figure of a man. She felt disorientated for a moment until she realised it was a stranger; someone who just reminded her of him.

Her mother was already preparing their meal when she got in. Jolly greeted her effusively in the hall and hurried to indicate where his lead dangled on the hallstand.

'Later, Jolly! Promise.' She went into the kitchen.

'Hello, love. How was it?'

Kate smiled.

'Fine. My feet ache, though!'

'Have you started looking for something else?'

'I checked the local paper this morning but there was nothing suitable. The weekend papers are more likely to have the kind of job I'd like. I'm also going to register at the local employmeny agency.'

'Good! Oh, by the way, a Mrs Hayes

phoned. She said she wanted to talk to you and would ring back later.'

'Mrs Hayes? That must be Ryan's mother. I wonder what she wants.'

The meal wasn't quite ready when the phone rang. Kate answered it.

'Kate? Hugh tells me you have quit your job. Why? He found your letter this morning and tried to phone you straight away, but there was no answer.

'He has to attend some dinner or other this evening. It is one of those dinners where there are endless speeches about things no-one is interested in, and everyone must deactivate their mobile phones.

'He begged me to call and persuade you to come back straight away. Hugh doesn't like asking me to do him a favour one little bit, so you can see how much he cares!

'Apparently, Ryan has gone tearing off to Paris and Hugh doesn't know why he went, or when he's coming back.

'Hugh was in a rebellious mood and

he was very agitated. I gather that it has something to do with Ryan's clients. He was blustering and so angry, it was hard to follow what he was getting at.

'I can't remember when he was last so furious about something. He kept telling me it was all Ryan's fault.'

Kate related what had happened calmly.

'I know that Hugh trusted me and that he didn't think I'd cheat the company, but I had the impression Ryan did.

'You can imagine that it's an impossible situation, if one of the partners suspects their secretary is a thief. Even if Ryan finds out who it was, it'll always be a barrier between him and me.'

'How absurd! I don't mean about what you think about the situation, I mean about the fact that Ryan could doubt you for a single minute.

'Are you sure that you have understood properly? Couldn't you go back and give them a chance to talk it over with you in peace and quiet? Hugh sounded so mad that I think he and Ryan might have an almighty row when he comes back.'

Kate laughed.

'Even if he was livid, I can't imagine Hugh shouting at anyone. He's such a mild and easy-going character. I can't go back, Mrs Hayes,' she added firmly. 'If I did, I'd need to work as if nothing had changed, but it has. I left without warning or giving them proper notice. Hugh won't mind that I did it that way, but Ryan is a stickler for the rules. I can't go back.'

'And what will you do?'

'Look for another job. I'm working temporarily in a bistro. That will keep my head above water until I find something more permanent.'

Mrs Hayes took an audible deep breath.

'In a bistro? Where is it? Are you mad? I don't believe this is all happening! Ryan mentioned you're a qualified accountant. You'll have no trouble finding a job with your qualifications.'

Kate chuckled. She could imagine the determined expression on his mother's face.

'Someone has to work in bistros. Mine is near the office, down a side street. Today was my first day. I like it. I'm getting to know all kinds of people.

'I do intend to look for something else of course, something that pays more, but at least I'm earning a little. It's better than sitting in the corner, doing nothing, and just worrying about what the future will bring.'

'I haven't the contacts I once had, but I will ask anyone I think might have a suitable job. This week, and particularly today, was full of good news for me until Hugh phoned. Now I feel dismayed. You were good for Hugh and for Ryan.'

Kate wanted Mrs Hayes to know she already knew about the engagement before she told Kate how happy she was about it.

'Well, at least you can look forward to the happy news, about Ryan and Louise.'

'Pardon? I was referring to the fact that the district manager of the organisation I work for, asked me if I'd like to organise and run a new branch they plan to open soon.

'I hope they can find some voluntary helpers in the area, otherwise I'd have too much to do, and Bernard might start kicking up a fuss about it.' She paused as the words sunk in. 'What do you mean — Ryan and Louise?'

'I met Louise the other day,' Kate said, flustered. 'She told me that she and Ryan are getting married, that they would announce their engagement soon.'

There was a deathly silence.

'I thought you knew. I hope I'm not jumping the gun! By the way, that's very good news about your job. It shows how well you are doing.'

'I certainly do not know anything about an engagement. I didn't even know that Ryan was in a serious relationship. Louise?'

'Yes, Louise Thalmy. You met her at Ryan's party. She dragged Ryan off to meet her brother.

'You mentioned you'd met her at the theatre with Ryan a few weeks previously. She was also among the guests at the company party down by the river.'

Mrs Hayes sighed with exasperation.

'Oh, that woman. And she and Ryan are getting engaged?' Mrs Hayes sighed. 'Things are getting worse by the minute today.

'I know that my two boys ignore my advice, but I can't imagine that Ryan would be engaged to anyone unless we'd met her officially beforehand. He's a cautious character, who isn't impulsive.

'I wouldn't be surprised if Anthony married a starlet in Las Vegas, or married without telling us, but Ryan . . . No, it's not how he acts.' She paused.

237

'On the other hand, I don't understand why he thought you were pinching information from the company, either. It seems I don't know my son very well at all.'

Kate could have added that she had thought she understood him too but now realised that she didn't, either.

'He's master of his own life. He knows what he's doing — at least I think he does,' she said instead.

'I hope so. If what you say is true, I'd better be careful what I think or say about this Louise woman. If she does turn out to be my daughter-in-law, I'll have to learn to curb my tongue.'

Kate laughed.

'If you want to keep a good relationship to your son, I think that would be a good idea! Thank you for phoning, and tell Hugh not to worry.

'I'll find something else, and he won't have as much trouble finding a replacement, either, because things are up to date in the office and tidy.

'Tell him to find someone fast then

238

he won't mess things up again too much before someone else takes over. I promise to ring him when I've settled somewhere else. I'll keep in touch — promise!'

'With me, too, I hope? I like you, Kate.'

'Thank you, that's kind of you. I like you too. I like people who are honest and direct.'

'Some people have trouble with that. I can't keep my mouth shut sometimes.'

Kate laughed.

'Bye, Mrs Hayes. Take care!'

'I will, and good luck with finding a job that suits. Bye, Kate!'

Arms and Hearts
Entwined

Next day, Kate felt a little better. Perhaps talking to Ryan's mother about Ryan's engagement had helped her realise that it was all over. She would phone Hugh one day, but not until she could listen to Ryan's name without a wave of sadness and regret.

After breakfast, she went to the local Job Centre and registered for a job seeker interview. When she returned home, her mother had left early for work. Kate took Jolly for a walk and then set off for the bistro.

Cynthia was busy clearing some tables when she arrived.

'Hi! Everything OK?' Kate asked.

Cynthia smiled.

'Not too bad.' She looked at the clock. 'You're dead on time. Good! I can fit in some shopping on the way home.' She bundled herself into her coat, and with a cheery farewell, she disappeared.

The trade was brisk all afternoon. Kate was busy and time passed quickly. She also noticed that the owner wasn't watching her every single movement like a hawk any more. That was a good sign.

After her shift was over, she stood outside for a moment enjoying the fresh air. A movement across the road caught her eye, where railings bordered a small recreation area. Someone was leaning casually against the fence and looking at her. She knew who it was before he'd straightened.

Her stomach churned. She turned away and began to hurry down the road. She guessed he would come after her, but she needed every second she could to adjust and be in control.

She wasn't surprised when he put his hand on her shoulder. She kept her features deceptively composed when she looked up at the man she still loved so much.

'What do you want?' she asked, managing to sound curt.

'If I don't do something to close the rift between us, my whole family is going to throw me to the lions,' he said in a matter of fact tone. He gave her a smile that sent her pulses racing.

'And if I don't do something soon I am also going to be more miserable than I've ever been before.'

She stiffened and reminded herself that he didn't trust her.

'How did you know where to find me, and why on earth are you bothering?'

'While she was tearing me off a strip, my mother mentioned you said the bistro was near the office. There aren't many in this area. I just checked them one by one until I found the right one. I spotted you working through the window.'

She spoke with quiet determination.

'What do you want, Ryan?' She reminded herself not to let his looks distract her but as their eyes met, she felt a shock run through her.

He glowered at her for a moment.

'I don't understand why you think I accused you of stealing. I didn't. Perhaps I should have said it loudly at the time and saved you and me all this confusion.

'You should know me well enough by now to know that I have the habit of concentrating on whatever task is in hand. At that particular moment, I was trying to figure out how I could trace the security leak.

'I didn't imagine you would take a lack of immediate verbal support in such a personal way,' he continued. 'Hugh reacted faultlessly, but I bungled the situation. I apologise sincerely. Of course I didn't think you were involved in stealing those names, not for a second.'

She glared at him.

'You talked about the two of you

being above suspicion, meaning yourself and Hugh,' she snapped. 'There was no mention of my name, and don't pretend you didn't notice my reaction.'

He ran his hand through his hair.

'I didn't notice — honestly. I understand why you quit if you thought I believed you were a thief. I'm totally, completely, utterly sorry, Kate. Please give me a chance to make it up to you.'

The silence between them became unbearable as she absorbed the words. She flushed miserably and finally nodded.

'OK, I accept your apology.'

'Thank heavens. By the way, I found out who was responsible — through an au pair on my list. I almost got her a job with a prominent film star in Paris when a rival agency jumped in at the last minute and placed her in exactly the same position.

'I asked her if she'd heard any pertinent conversation and she said she'd heard the name Thalmy during a phone call when she was sitting opposite the rival agent in his office.'

Kate spluttered.

'Thalmy, Louise Thalmy? But . . . '

Amusement flickered in his eyes.

'Yes, Miss Thalmy. The same Miss Thalmy that you told my mother was my future fiancée. Why anyone believes I'd ever fancy Louise, I don't understand.

'When I confronted Louise and asked her if she'd done it, she finally gave in and admitted she'd stolen a list from my desk once when I wasn't there, and another time out of my briefcase during my party invitation.

'She didn't say why she did it or why she lied about an engagement, but I can make a guess.'

Kate could remember when Louise had been in his office on her own.

'What do you believe?'

He shrugged.

'I think she can't accept that any other women could be more attractive or more interesting. She was continually contacting me about invitations, asking about where I was, what I was doing, and with whom.

'It was getting quite annoying. We both know a lot of the same people, so I couldn't completely avoid her. She didn't want to accept I wasn't interested in her. Why me, I don't know because I never gave her any encouragement.

'She noticed that I was more than just interested in you from the very first day. She was jealous, and wanted you out of the way.

She thought if she could get you into trouble by pinching important office information and passing it on to a rival agency you would automatically get the blame. In a way, it was extremely clever how she did it.'

'Me? But she had no reason to be jealous.'

'There was — because she saw how I was falling in love with you. She probably hoped she and I would end up together, but my fate was sealed the day we met. I know how I feel about you, but I don't know what you feel about me. I do love you — a fact that Louise noticed straight away.'

Kate shook her head in utter disbelief and looked up at his face. Excitement and blank amazement grew inside as he reached forward for her. She didn't resist and he held her snugly.

'This is where you belong,' he said softly. 'How could you believe I would ever want to hurt you, when I love you more than anything or anyone else on this earth?'

He claimed her lips and crushed her to him. Her knees weakened and she savoured every moment. She managed to struggle back to reality.

'And what will you do about Louise?' she asked.

He kissed the tip of her nose.

'Forget all about Louise.' He smiled. 'We have what she'll never have. We can pity her. I've warned her if she steps out of line with you or me ever again, that I'll go to her father.' Amusement flickered in his eyes. 'Her father would probably reduce her allowance, and that's worse than a slow death for Louise. I don't think we'll see much of her ever again.'

Kate took a deep breath as he slipped his arms around her again.

'You haven't said you love me,' he pointed out. 'I have a feeling you do, but please tell me so.'

Her whole face lit up in a smile.

'Of course I do. I can't believe this is happening. This isn't some kind of cheap trick just to get me back behind that desk, in that office, I hope.'

He laughed, and then picked her up to swing her around. He kissed her again.

'What do you think?'

She appraised his features closely.

'Do you know something?' she said softly. 'I don't care. If you do want me back in that office, or if you wanted me to go to the ends of the earth, I'd go.'

'Most of all, I want you with me. Hugh will be delighted if you come back, and even more so, when I tell him you're my girl. I admitted to my mother that I was in love with you and she was as pleased as I've ever seen her. You haven't met my father yet, but you will as soon as possible. Anthony will be very pleased because he knows I love you. I can only hope your mother will be happy.'

He paused.

'We are now going out to celebrate, and we'll sort the rest out later.'

She tried to control her emotions.

'Ryan, we don't know each other very well. Perhaps it won't last.'

He shook his head decisively.

'It will. I've never felt like this about any other woman before. I'm longing to show you just how much I love you, from this moment on.' He tilted his head. 'Perhaps you'll be looking for somewhere new to live soon, whenever your mother feels she can cope with the situation on her own. I have the perfect solution, and I'll even find somewhere to hang Edward's picture.'

Kate coloured and smiled. She had

never felt so blissfully happy and fully alive.

'I do love you, very, very, much.'

He nodded.

'We have the present and we'll have the rest of our lives to love each other. I'll be grateful for each and every day we are together.' He held her close and she felt the strength of his body. 'I can't imagine life without you any more. Let's go to Paris this weekend. I want to make up for the mess I made of it last time you were there, and Paris is the city of romance and lovers. What do you say?'

She nodded, her eyes sparkling.

'That is a brilliant idea.'

Arms and hearts entwined, they wandered on, each in the delight of knowing they belonged to each other at last.